ALSO BY SUSAN FLETCHER

Falcon in the Glass
Alphabet of Dreams
Walk Across the Sea
Shadow Spinner

THE DRAGON CHRONICLES
Dragon's Milk
Flight of the Dragon Kyn
Sign of the Dove
Ancient, Strange, and Lovely

JOURNEY
OF THE
PALE BEAR

S U S A N F L E T C H E R

Margaret K. McElderry Books
New York   London   Toronto   Sydney   New Delhi

MARGARET K. McELDERRY BOOKS
An imprint of Simon & Schuster Children's Publishing Division
1230 Avenue of the Americas, New York, New York 10020
This book is a work of fiction. Any references to historical events, real people,
or real places are used fictitiously. Other names, characters, places, and events
are products of the author's imagination, and any resemblance to actual events or
places or persons, living or dead, is entirely coincidental.
Text copyright © 2018 by Susan Fletcher
Jacket illustration copyright © 2018 by Shane Rebenschied
All rights reserved, including the right of reproduction in whole or in part in any
form.
MARGARET K. McELDERRY BOOKS is a trademark of Simon & Schuster, Inc.
For information about special discounts for bulk purchases,
please contact Simon & Schuster Special Sales at 1-866-506-1949 or
business@simonandschuster.com.
The Simon & Schuster Speakers Bureau can bring authors to your live event. For
more information or to book an event, contact the Simon & Schuster Speakers
Bureau at 1-866-248-3049 or visit our website at
www.simonspeakers.com.
Book design by Debra Sfetsios-Conover
The text for this book was set in Weiss STD.
Manufactured in the United States of America
0818 FFG
First Edition
10 9 8 7 6 5 4 3 2 1
Library of Congress Cataloging-in-Publication Data
Names: Fletcher, Susan, 1951– author.
Title: Journey of the pale bear / Susan Fletcher.
Description: First Edition. | New York : Margaret K. McElderry Books, [2018] |
Summary: Twelve-year-old Arthur forms a bond with a polar bear given by King
Haakon IV of Norway to King Henry III of England in 1252 while traveling as
her handler. Includes historical notes.
Identifiers: LCCN 2017049316 (print) | ISBN 9781534420779 (hardcover) |
ISBN 9781534420793 (eBook) |
Subjects: | CYAC: Human-animal relationships—Fiction. | Polar bear—
Fiction. | Bears—Fiction. | Adventure and adventurers—Fiction. |
Voyages and travels—Fiction. | Great Britain—History—Henry III, 1216–
1272—Fiction.
Classification: LCC PZ7.F6356 Jou 2018 (print) | DDC [Fic]—dc23
LC record available at https://lccn.loc.gov/2017049316

≋ FOR QUINCE ≋

Prologue

London, 1272

IN THE EVENING, as darkness falls, I return to the fortress. A guard lifts a lantern to my face, and at once I'm blind, blinking against the flood of sudden brightness. A jingle of chain mail, the clank of a sword . . . The lantern moves aside, and dusk flows back, save for the specks of phantom light that swim through the air before me. I hear the great iron bolts scrape in their housings; I hear the rusty *thunk* as they break free. Then the high western gate clears its throat and rasps open to admit me.

One of the guards peels off from the others to lead me; they all know where I am going. Our footfalls clunk hollowly on the wooden bridge across the moat. A second gate heaves open; we enter the corridors of the outer bailey, wading through eddies of light and shadow cast by the guard's swinging lantern. The leather harness is familiar in my hand. The rope is heavy on my shoulder; its great, thick coils creak softly as we walk. By and by, I pick up the dusty scent of feathers, a whiff of matted fur, the earthy perfume of dung. I hear a shifting of hooves, a snort, a growl, a yawn . . . and then a deep, familiar chuff of greeting.

The bear is waiting, pressed up against the bars, her old nose twitching. She always smells me coming, though how she does so is a mystery, for now the reek of her is filling me up with a deep, sharp, musky odor that leaves no room for other smells. The key grates in the lock; the guard ducks behind me; I slip within the cage.

The bear snuffles me all over and then presents her great wide head for me to scratch—her left ear with the notch from where the pirate slashed her; her snout with the arrow's pitted scar. I set down the harness and dig all ten fingers deep, clear down to the black of her skin, the way she likes. Her fur is thick and coarse. I bury my face in it and breathe the still-wild scent of her. She makes a sound, then: a low, rumbling sigh that tunnels up from the heart of the earth.

I slip the harness over her head and buckle it at her chest. I take the rope from my shoulder and fasten it to the harness ring. I lead her out of her cage, beneath the trees of the Tower Green, toward the water gate.

She is an old bear now. Her coat is dull, most of her teeth are gone, and her hip bones jut like fins above her back. She shuffles behind me, stiff with age, and limping—docile as one of the lambs on my stepfather's steading. She no longer craves escape; at long last, she seems content.

But it was not always so. Once, she struck fear into the hearts of hardened sailors, swam for leagues in the sea without stopping, withstood a hail of arrows, waged battle against pirates, rescued a boy who had come to love her, and was flaunted and prized by kings. Once long ago . . . when she and I were young.

PART I

NORWAY

≋ CHAPTER I ≋

Thief

Bergen, Norway
Spring, 1252

IT WAS THE smell of roasting meat that roused me.

A small rain had begun to fall, and though I had curled up beneath the eaves of a cobbler's shop, the ground soaked up the damp and wicked it through my cloak and tunic, into my shirt. Now a wave of talk and laughter met my ear, but I knew that wasn't what had wakened me.

No, it was the smell.

It teased me, growing stronger and then fainter—so faint I thought, for a moment, that I had dreamed it. But then it was back again, a rich, deep, meaty aroma that set all the waters in my mouth to flowing. I rose to one elbow and breathed it in, imagining tearing into a hunk of my mother's roasted mutton, feeling the warmth of it going down and the heavy, drowsy ease of a full belly.

I straightened my cap on my head, hitched my knapsack to my shoulder, and wobbled to my feet. It had been two days since I had finished the last of my provisions, and hunger had made me weak.

The voices dimmed and then swelled again. It was dark; even the stars had vanished. The crowds had thinned, and the men who passed me now seemed somehow sinister, their faces distorted by the shadows of the lanterns that had begun to flicker to life. Beyond the quays the shops and houses of Bergen stood resolutely shoulder to shoulder, solid and prosperous, leaving no room for a starveling waif such as I.

I crept down the street and rounded a corner into an alley, where I spied an inn before me, light blazing from its windows. The rich fragrance of meat assailed me more powerfully than before, flooding my nose and mouth and throat. I told myself that it was fruitless to torture myself with tantalizing aromas. That, without coin, I would be unwelcome in a place such as this. That I might even find myself in peril.

I pushed open the door. I stepped within.

The inn was dim and crowded, rank with the commingled odors of sweat and sour ale and wet wool and mud. But the smell of warm meat wafted all about and underneath the other smells, and it lured me in deep. A serving maid brushed past me bearing a tray above her head. She slapped it down on a table: a mound of roasted rabbit sitting in a puddle of gravy and blood. Men in blue, sailor's garb thronged in about it, digging in with hands and knives. The meat vanished from the platter so quickly it was hard to credit, until a single leg joint lay there alone.

I didn't think; I moved.

I slipped between two seamen who were reaching for it, snatched up the rabbit haunch, and ran hard for the door.

A shout: "Hey! You, boy!" Then more shouts, and curses, and a scraping of benches behind me. "Halt, thief!"

Someone seized my cloak from behind, nearly toppling me. I twisted round and laid eyes on him—a blond, brawny sailor of maybe fifteen years; maybe three years older than I. I kicked his shin and then tore myself away. I scrambled up onto a table and stumbled toward the other side, knocking over a row of flagons and a pitcher of ale.

"Hey!"

Hands reached for my legs. I dodged, stumbling into a trencher full of meat, then leaped from the table and made for the door. I pushed it open. Knocked into a man coming in. Slipped and fell to the ground— all without releasing my grip on the rabbit haunch. I scrambled to my feet and headed into the darkness, praying that the sailors behind me would be too lazy or too drunk to follow.

CHAPTER 2

Feral

I BOLTED DOWN the street, skidded round a corner, and turned into an alley. I could hear them coming— heavy footsteps, the clink of something iron. I cast a quick look over my shoulder and saw that one of them had a lantern.

I crossed a grassy lane, hurtled around another corner, found myself at a crossroads, spotted another alley, and ducked into that.

Ahead, I saw a wide door standing ajar. A blue-clad seaman and a woman huddled together a little way down the alley, the man's head bent toward the woman's hair. I heard the woman giggle, then I slowed to a walk so as not to call notice to myself. I looked behind me. I could still hear footsteps, faintly, but couldn't tell where they came from, and I didn't see the men who had been following.

I slipped through the doorway.

Even darker, here. Some kind of warehouse. It smelled strongly of fish, but an odd, animal smell wafted in to me, as well. Not horse, not sheep, not cow, but . . . My toe knocked against something hard. I reached down and felt the rounded surface of a barrel. I crept a little way within so that I couldn't be seen from the door.

Then I crouched and began to eat. I tore at the rabbit haunch with my teeth, the juices running down my chin, into my tunic and shirt. Meat! Still warm, and—

Voices. Two men burst into the room behind me. I scrambled to avoid the skinny one with the lantern and slammed straight into the other. I recognized him— the blond boy-man from the tavern. He took me by the scruff of my cloak. "I'll teach you to steal from me, you—" I felt a tug at my knapsack. "Well, what have we here?"

A certain tone in his voice reminded me of my eldest stepbrother, Edvin, when he wanted something that was mine. I tried to twist away, but the sailor held me fast.

A low rumble sounded from a dark corner of the warehouse. Hair rose on the nape of my neck; the man froze.

"What's that?" the one with the lantern asked. He seemed young, not much older than I.

"Don't know," said the other. He seized my wrist—hard. "Why don't we find out?"

"Let's flee this place, Hauk," the lantern boy said. "You can rough him up in the alley."

"Stop your sniveling," the one called Hauk said. "I want to see what's what."

Another rumble, and the shuffling, scraping sound of a heavy footfall. The prospect of being roughed up in an alley was beginning to sound good. My step-brothers roughed me up all the time. I was expert at being roughed up. I kicked Hauk's shin—twice—but then he belly-punched me, and I doubled over from the pain. He moved deeper into the warehouse, dragging me behind. The animal smell grew stronger—feral and sharp with musk—a smell that boded ill.

By the dim glow of the lantern, I made out a large, pale form in the gloom. An animal . . . in a cage.

A bear. An ice bear, from the north.

It paced from one end of its cage to the other and then back again, shaking its head with an impatient twitchy restlessness, a restlessness I knew well, the kind that hums and jangles loud inside, until every sinew in your body is coiled spring-tight and craves only to run, run far away.

"Hauk," the lantern boy said, "let's go."

But Hauk was dragging me toward the bear. I saw what he intended to do now and struggled to get loose. I yelled, I kicked, I beat at him with the rabbit haunch. He tore my knapsack from my shoulder, then grasped both of my arms and pinned them behind me.

The bear let out a long breath, a sort of moan.

"No," I said. "Don't do it. I'll give you back your meat, I'll—"

But Hauk turned me sideways and began to stuff me between the bars. At first I thought I wouldn't fit, but then my shoulders slipped partway through, and then my head, and then my hips. I staggered into the cage and, tripping, slammed my knees against the floor.

When I looked up, the bear had gone still at the far end of the cage. It was staring straight at me.

⃰ CHAPTER 3 ⃰

Ice Bear

ITS EYES, SMALL and dark, were alert, curious, aware.
I felt the faint stirring of its breath against my cheeks.
I drew in the rich, ripe scent of *bear* until I seemed to
sink down below the surface of it, drowning. From
somewhere far away I heard Hauk and the lantern boy
arguing, but the sounds fell away behind the throbbing of my bloodbeat in my ears and the thrill of the
running-hum in my limbs.

The bear rumbled deep in its throat.

I rose to my feet, stepped back, and felt the iron
bars press cold against me. I kept my eyes fixed on
the pale, wide face, as if the force of my gaze could

prevent the bear from lunging at me with its enormous jaws or raking me with its claws—claws that I could see out of the corners of my eyes, massive claws, claws from a nightmare of monsters.

Twitching. The big black nose was twitching, snuffling, searching. There was a thrumming in the air that came to lodge within my bones and sang there. Slowly, the bear's head reached toward me, and I saw there was something loose and flapping off one shoulder—a harness. And then the dark eyes shifted away from mine to peer at the center of my chest. I looked down and saw my fingers clutched round the rabbit haunch. That's what the bear was sniffing. Carefully, I moved the meat away from my chest. It seemed that I might just hold it out and offer it, as you would hand a dropped thimble to your mother. But the bear took a step closer, and I felt a spasm of fear jolt through me. I tossed the haunch as hard as I could, off to one side. It smacked against the bars and hit the floor of the cage with a splat.

For the merest instant, the bear's expression shifted. The great head swiveled to gaze straight into my eyes with something like reproach—seeming to say that it hadn't been necessary to throw the food, that that had been beneath the bear's dignity and mine.

Then it turned, snatched up the rabbit leg in its great jaws, and snapped it in twain.

I let out my breath in a rush. I felt behind me with one foot and slipped it between the bars. I could hear voices, but nobody stopped me. The bear was making a terrible racket, cracking bones, gnashing and slurping. The haunch wouldn't last much longer, and then . . . Slowly, I pushed backward until my hips slid through, and I was in the midst of trying to squeeze my chest and shoulders between the bars when a new, deeper voice called out, "You there! Boy!"

The bear lifted its head and roared. I tried to shove my shoulders backward between the bars, but I was doing it amiss; I was stuck. Then someone was pulling me, pulling on my hand. I popped between the bars, but too fast—I hadn't turned my head—and I cracked my chin against hard iron. "Hurry!" the new voice said. I swiveled my head and slipped it through just as the bear came down against the side of the cage with a crash that made the bars shudder and quaked the very floor beneath my feet.

The bear roared again, throwing my thoughts into a dim and galloping confusion. I felt the hand release mine; I heard a scuffle behind me; I heard shouts. The roar ceased. I blinked, looked about me, and began to slip away toward the door—but then a hand closed around my arm, and the deep voice boomed in my ear:

"Have you taken leave of your senses? What were you doing in there?"

≋ CHAPTER 4 ≋

This One We'll Keep

I COULDN'T SEE him well in the flickering gloom, but I sensed a squareness, a firmness, a solidity about this man. His hand clamped onto my arm, like a ring of iron, and I knew it would be useless to try to escape. "What have you to say for yourself?" he demanded.

I looked about me and found Hauk, whose hands, I saw, had been bound behind him. A tail of rope led from Hauk's wrists and into the clenched fist of the seaman I'd seen with the woman outside. He must be a guard—one who'd been distracted from his duty.

"He pushed me into the cage," I said, pointing at

Hauk. "I was just going about my business, and—"

"He stole my supper!" Hauk said.

"Did not!"

"Did so!"

"Did not!"

"Did so! I have witnesses!"

The man who held me turned to Hauk. "I suppose your witness would be the boy who got away?" he asked.

"That's Ottar," Hauk said. "Go to the inn, the Brass Dwarf. They'll know where to find him. And others saw too. They'll tell you, same as me."

I swallowed, recalling how I had jumped up onto the table, kicking over flagons and trampling food. Yes, there were witnesses aplenty.

"But," the man said to Hauk, "you broke in here, where you don't belong, and beleaguered the bear—"

Beleaguered *the bear*? What about me?

"I didn't break in," Hauk said. "The door was open. And *he* came here first." Hauk jerked his head in my direction. "I was just following."

"And you thrust him into the bear cage for his trouble?"

Hauk shrugged. "I let him out again, didn't I?"

"He could have been killed. Very nearly was—or at

least"—the man turned to regard me with curiosity—
"that's my thinking at present."

"I *was*. I was almost killed," I said. "And he stole my
knapsack!" I pointed to where it lay on the floor. "And
he didn't *let* me out, he—"

"And *did* you steal his supper?"

My face grew warm. For a moment it had begun to
seem as if the man might take my part. What did they
do to thieves here in the city, I wondered. Lock them
up? Banish them? Cut off their hands?

The man's grip tightened. "Did you?"

"I didn't know it was his," I mumbled.

"But you stole it!" Hauk said.

"I was hungry. Somebody robbed me, took all my
coins!"

"Hmm." The man eyed me for a moment, as if calcu-
lating the length of rope he would need to hang me.

"What do you want me to do with this one, Doctor?"
the guard asked, giving Hauk's leash a yank.

Doctor. I had deemed him a constable or some
other high-ranking official.

"You stay far away from here," the doctor told
Hauk. "I don't care what the other one has stolen. If I
catch you anywhere *near* the bear again, you'll be very
sorry indeed."

15

"What about him?" Hauk demanded, glaring at me. "Never mind about him. You stay away. Understood?"

Hauk shrugged.

"Is that understood?"

"Yes." It came out grudgingly, between clamped teeth.

"Wait," the doctor said. "You said the Brass Dwarf. You're a seaman?"

Hauk shrugged again. The guard yanked hard on the rope. Hauk stumbled, bleated out, "Yes!"

"Where are you bound?"

"Why do you want to—"

Yank.

"London."

London. I had tried to get hired on that ship, but they wouldn't have me.

The doctor said nothing for a moment. Then: "Release him," he said.

"But—" the guard protested.

"I doubt he'll be back."

The guard whipped out a knife and sliced through Hauk's bindings, then gave him a quick boot to the backside. Hauk disappeared into the darkness.

"And this one?" the guard asked, nodding at me.

"Oh, this one," the doctor said. "This one we'll keep."

CHAPTER 5

The Brass Dwarf

HE TOOK ME to the inn, the Brass Dwarf, the same one as before. He returned my knapsack and promised to feed me—said he wanted to talk to me. I feared he might round up Hauk's witnesses and then turn me over to the constabulary to . . . what? Put me in the stocks? Blind me in one eye? Draw and quarter me? I considered giving him a shove and trying to break out of his grasp, but his grip tightened around my arm, as if he could sense what I was thinking, and I knew that for now I could not escape.

A din rose about us as we entered. The smell of ale wafted through the air, mingling with the aromas of meat and sweat, and a thick haze of smoke hung over all. Clearly, the drink had had its effect, for now there was singing, there was dancing, there was stomping in time to a foreign piper's air. Two seamen carried on a mock-fight in the middle of the floor and, not far from that, two others out-and-out brawled—biting, poking at eyes, grabbing for hair and ears. The light was dim, and to my relief, no one seemed to recognize me as the rabbit thief. In fact, I didn't think anyone even gave me a glance. The doctor threaded through gaps in the close-pressed crowd. At last he motioned me to sit at a far back table, where the clamor subsided to a dreary roar.

He called for a meal—a trencher of barley bread topped with a thick venison stew—and pushed it across the table to me when it came. I shrugged off my knapsack, withdrew my knife and my spoon from its case, and tucked in forthwith, fearful that my supper might be taken away at any moment, and wanting to get as much inside me as I could. The meat was tough, with many chunks of gristle, but soon my belly began to feel warm and full. I drilled down to the last soggy bits of gravy-soaked bread, and then there was nothing for it but to look back up again, where I found the doctor gazing at me.

He had a wide, squarish face—not plump, but a sturdy, big-boned kind of wide. His eyes, sharp and alert, reminded me of the eyes of the put-to-pasture warhorse my stepfather once had—ever vigilant against danger, yet still with the sad, weary wisdom of one who has seen too much of suffering and of death. By the light of the smoking candle stub on our table, I could see the tiny pits and scars that pocked the doctor's cheeks, and the wrinkles that fanned out from the corners of his eyes and etched wavy lines in his brow. He neither smiled nor frowned, but regarded me as if I were a riddle to be solved.

"How long since last you ate?" he asked.

I shrugged.

"Where is your father?"

The question conjured his voice—my father's—the deep, warm gravel of it. It was six years since the fever had taken him, when I was six years old.

I shrugged again.

"Very well, your mother. Where is she?"

Mother . . . She would be desperate with worry. She wouldn't know if I was alive or dead.

"So you're a runaway, then?"

I felt the familiar restless energy begin to build up in my legs, felt it thrumming in my blood. I braced one hand against the table and one foot on the rush-strewn floor. What did they do to runaways in this city? Cut off their toes? Keep them as slaves? Boil them in oil?

But when I glanced at the doctor, something about the way he looked at me . . . held me. It was not as you would look at a too-small, worthless boy who had run away from home yet again, but as you might look at a hammer to see if it was well wrought before you laid down good coin for it.

"Very well, then," the doctor said after a moment, "I'll ask you something else. Do you have a way with animals? With horses or dogs or cows or . . . whatever animals you've found yourself among?"

The bear. This was about the bear.

I quickly said "No," as the fear surged up in a sour rush from the pit of my stomach. On the steading, we knew about ice bears. Hunters dropped by, telling stories . . . We feared ice bears above wolves and lynxes—above all other beasts.

The doctor's gaze did not leave my face. "Because," he went on, as if I had said nothing at all, "it seemed to me that you did have a way with that bear. When I first came into the warehouse, she was only *looking* at you. Sniffing at you, it seemed. How long were you in there? She has attacked everyone who has tried to feed her or clean her cage . . . save for you."

She. I hadn't thought of the bear as a *she*, and yet . . .

"You can't make me go back there. I won't go back in that cage again—not ever!"

"If someone has to go in there with her, it'll be me, not you. But if your presence outside the cage could calm her, that would be a boon. She's been pacing day and night, flinging herself against the bars. The men are afraid even to go near her, and she . . . Well. She's not overly fond of me either." He rolled up his sleeve to show a deep, ridged slash on his forearm, scabbed over but red at the edges. "I tried to stupefy her with sleeping herbs so I could work with her, but they didn't take. And even if they did . . . She's not eating enough to stay alive. So someone she tolerates, someone with a way with animals, might smooth the path for us all."

"Why?" I asked. "Why do you care about a bear?"

"I don't give a rat's shinbone for that bear!" The doctor cleared his throat and seemed to collect himself; when he spoke again, the anger had ebbed from his voice. "But I'm bound to keep her well, for reasons that are none of your concern. And so . . . Do you, boy? Do you have a way with animals? If you do, and if you can help, I'll make it worth your while."

It was true that some of the farm animals were drawn to me. The byre cats rubbed against my legs and purred—even old Baldur, who only hissed at everybody else. Sheep came to graze near me when I was chinking the fence. Once, when the cows broke into the home fields, I called them and led them back where they belonged, easy as pie. My father had had a way with horses, and I too knew how to put them at their ease.

But the bear . . .

I remembered the running energy I had sensed on her, echoing the restlessness I often felt. I recalled the look she gave me when I threw the rabbit haunch, the look of reproach . . .

"What will become of her?" I asked. "If you want her for her pelt . . ."

"I don't. We don't."

"What, then?"

"She is not mine. She is . . . a gift. From one very powerful man to another."

"Are you a powerful man?"

"No. I serve a powerful man."

"But who would want a live bear?"

"Listen . . . What did you say your name was?"

I hadn't. But I said it to him now. "Arthur."

"Listen, Arthur. The powerful do as they will; it's fruitless for the likes of us to try to fathom their ways. But I have two questions for you: What do *you* want? What can I do for you in payment for your aid?"

I gaped at him. No one had ever asked me such questions before.

"Would you like me to find you a patron and a secure home? Would you like me to apprentice you in a trade? These are in my power. I could return you to your mother and father, if—"

"My father's dead."

Something flashed across the doctor's face—a quick spasm. Behind me, I heard the clank of crockery, a sudden roar of laughter.

"What do you want?" the doctor asked again, and his voice was softer than before.

I felt a prickling behind my eyes. I frowned and clamped my jaws together.

What did I want?

Mother. I want to go home.

But no. I had run from the tyranny of my stepfather, from the constant, petty cruelties of my stepbrothers. In truth, I had been running from them for years. The familiar restlessness would build to a twitchy hum that jangled in my limbs until I couldn't sit, couldn't stand, couldn't keep to my chores—until I had no choice in the matter but to run, run away. To the boathouse on the fjord. To the caves high in the fells. I would hold out there for as long as I could, until hunger drove me back, or loneliness, or cold. Then I would drag myself home, defeated, for there was nowhere, in truth, for me to go.

Until the letter came. The letter from my father's kin.

I drew in breath, sinking deep into memory, and found him there again—my father—smelling of sweat and leather and hay, setting me up before him on a shaggy pony, teaching me. *Hold the reins like so, my son. Sit up tall and cling tight with your legs. One day you and I will ride into battle with the prince.* I could feel my father's reassuring bulk behind me; I could feel the pony's coarse mane beneath my fingers; I could feel both of them warm and breathing.

"We leave on the morrow for London," the doctor said. "If you come with us, and if you tend to the bear until we arrive, I'll fetch you back to Bergen and give you what you want, if it's in my power."

London. "You're bound for London?"

The creases eased from the doctor's brow; he leaned

24

in toward me. "Do you want to go to London?"

I laid a hand on my knapsack, still on my lap, and felt the stiffness of parchment underneath. The letter. The letter from Wales. "Not to stay," I said. "But to go on from there to Wales. My father's kin are there, and they want me."

CHAPTER 6

The Letter

IT WAS THE farrier who gave it into my mother's hand. He had received it from the tinker, who had received it from a carter, who had received it from a ship's captain, come all the way from England the previous fall.

The farrier could read a little. He could make out my mother's name on the outside of the letter, and the name of the nearest town, which had been written, he'd said, in two different hands.

"I could try to parse it out," he had suggested.

My mother smoothed the letter with her fingers— thick, creamy-hued parchment, sealed with wax. She swept a lock of yellow hair from her eyes. I didn't know what she would do. She tended to keep things to herself, and this was none of the farrier's concern. But if she didn't let him read it, I knew we would have to wait for the priest, who wouldn't be by for at least another week. And my stepfather . . . He might take the letter from her, deeming it to be his by marital right, promising to have it read to *him* and to tell her what she needed to know.

By now, the occasion had begun to draw a crowd. I couldn't remember a letter ever having been brought to the steading before, though I knew that my stepfather kept two or three of them stowed in a small, locked chest. It was just after the midday meal, and though my stepfather was away buying a new brood mare, my three stepbrothers had gathered round, and a scattering of servants stood in a wider ring about us. Dogs milled about, sniffing, hoping for scraps; old Loki sat at my feet, leaning his grizzled head against my knee.

At last my mother tore her gaze from the letter and looked at the farrier with an urgency I had seldom seen in her. "Yes," she said, her voice low and tremulous. "Read it to me. Please."

"Let me see it," my stepbrother Edvin said. My mother lifted her head to look at him, then scanned the throng, hesitating.

Edvin leaned forward and reached for the letter, but my mother turned her shoulder to him, thrust the letter at the farrier, and repeated, "Read it."

Edvin's face reddened; he scowled. The farrier broke the seal and, with a sense of ceremony, unfolded the stiff paper.

He squinted. Brought the letter up close to his eyes. Held it out with arms straight. At last he turned to my mother. "What language this is, I cannot tell. Not ours, that's certain. It may be French, or possibly Latin, though it doesn't look right for those either. I've never seen the like."

He returned it to my mother. She studied it, one finger tracing its way down the parchment surface. The finger halted. "I know this word," she whispered. She glanced at me, then back down at the letter. "I've seen it on . . . on a stone."

She put one arm around me and brought the letter close with her other hand for me to see. She pointed at the word. "Look, Arthur," she said. "It's your father's name: Morcan. This letter harks from Wales."

\\\\\\

The next day, before my stepfather returned, my mother and I had sat side-by-side near the hearth and pored over the letter together. From time to time my stepbrothers had appeared—Edvin, then Halvdan, then Soren—demanding a cup of ale, a bannock, a hunk of cheese. She satisfied them quickly and then returned to the letter and to me.

Near the top of the parchment was the year, in numbers—1251—which both of us could read. And my mother showed me how to find *Morcan*, which appeared four more times. He had been a nobleman, my father—boon companion and master of the horse to Prince David. They had died of the selfsame illness, less than a week apart. My mother had never mastered the Welsh tongue, had never felt at home there. She was from a well-to-do Norwegian family, though not of noble blood. After my father died, my mother and I returned to Norway, and she remarried within the year.

Now, she pointed to another group of letters that repeated a number of times. "I think this is *you*," she said, hovering her finger over the word. "I think this must say 'Arthur.'"

"Why?" I asked her, stroking Baldur, who had come to purr on my lap. "Why would they write about me?"

The first time I asked, she gave me a quick, sharp look and seemed about to respond, but then tightened her lips about her words and held them in. The second time I asked, she ventured, "There was some land. Your birthright. But who knows if they've kept it for you?" The third time, she folded the letter, pointed to the door, and ordered me off to my work in the fields.

By the time my stepfather showed the letter to the priest, who said he couldn't read it either, I had cobbled together my own story about what the letter said and why it had been sent. I didn't know if someone had died in Wales, or if someone was about to die. I didn't know if it was because I had newly turned twelve and come into manhood, or some other circumstance—a fresh outbreak of war between Wales and England, perhaps. But as the days passed, I had become more and more certain that they wanted me and needed me—that they had summoned me back to Wales to help train the royal horses and ride with the young princes, to claim my birthright as my father's only son and heir.

⇒ CHAPTER 7 ⇐

Treacherous Pot

NOW THE DOCTOR stood, asking me to wait for him at the table. The captain, he said, was staying in a room upstairs; the doctor would confer with him and return forthwith to fetch me. If the captain said aye, I could lodge this very night on shipboard with the crew.

And after that I would only have to feed and clean up after the bear on the way to London.

Only!

The doctor, maybe sensing my hesitation, hastened to reassure me. "You can do all of it from well outside the cage, using long-handled brooms and rakes. You'll be safe. You have my word on it." But I was harking back to the smell of the bear, and her great, dark claws, and the stir of her breath on my cheeks. I remembered her roar, and the savage crunch of bones as she ate, and the deep red slash on the doctor's arm.

The doctor took his leave, and not for the first time, I wondered if I should have stayed on the steading, where at least I was well-fed and had a roof over my head. But I was of no consequence there to anyone save for my mother—and never would be.

I tucked my knife and spoon back into my knapsack and held it on my lap. The din of the tavern began to lose its sharp edges; it wove itself into a soft blanketing rumble that muffled all the sounds within it. The restlessness trickled out of me, leaving me heavy and limp and warm. My eyelids dragged shut; I blinked them open. I crossed my arms on the table, laid my head atop, and abandoned myself to a flood of uneasy memories.

\\|//

I couldn't have said when it began, but for many years I had had the sense of being shipwrecked in life—of having fetched up on a strange shore among wrong, unfitting people. There was nowhere to hide from the wrestling games I always lost and the horse-fights I abhorred and the drowning games that nearly killed me. I would never win my stepbrothers' good regard, nor that of my stepfather. I was smaller than they, and darker, favoring my Welsh father over my mother.

I had asked my stepfather to let me help train his horses, but he'd said I was too small for such work, and besides, he had long ago reserved that job for Halvdan. I had asked to work with any animals at all, but my stepfather had grudged me even that. He'd sent me to cut rushes or fell timber or mend fences with his servants, who didn't need my help either.

And so I ran away, in the wee hours before dawn on a bitter-cold May morning in the year of Our Lord 1252. In a cloth knapsack, I put the letter from Wales, my ashwood spoon and spooncase, and a small, sharp knife. I filched two pennies from under the board in the floor where my stepfather kept them, resolving to pay them back somehow. From the larder, I took a hunk of cheese, some strips of dried meat, and a bannock. Enough, I hoped, to sustain me on the journey to Bergen. From there, I hoped to find a ship bound for Wales . . . and a new life.

I knew it would have eased my mother's mind if I had told her my plans instead of stealing off into the night. But I had feared she would weep and try to dissuade me. And I longed to be of consequence—*to ride with the princes,* to find a valued place for myself in the world of men. I resolved to commission a letter for Mama later, when I was settled with my father's family.

I walked until sunrise, then climbed undetected into the back of a southbound tinker's cart. When, late that morning, the cart slowed near an inn, I jumped off and soon stowed away in an apothecary's wagon.

On the afternoon of the fourth day—after many leagues afoot and nine different carts and wagons—I rode into the port of Bergen in a pony cart, hidden beneath a mound of skinned pelts of hares and foxes. My head throbbed from lack of sleep; my feet sprouted blisters; and my back ached from slipping and jouncing over muddy, rutted roads.

I slipped off the back of the cart and made for the harbor.

But none of the shipmasters wanted a small-for-his-age cabin boy with nary a lick of experience. Soon all my food was gone, and a cutpurse had made off with my pennies. I might have given up and dragged myself back to the steading in disgrace, except I knew I'd likely starve on the long way home.

\\//

Now the sound of nearby voices roused me, and the scrape of boots on the floor. I looked up to see a band of seamen clambering onto the benches beside and across from me. "The table's ours, boy," one said. "If you want to sleep, go find yourself a bed."

"But I was here first," I protested.

A roar of laughter. A shove. And I sprawled out on the floor among the rushes.

I picked up my knapsack, slung the tie strings over one shoulder, and staggered to my feet.

The crowd in the tavern had grown rowdier, more drunken. Some of the sailors still danced, but they did not even feign keeping time with the music; they lurched and stumbled and reeled. I sidestepped to avoid a foul-tongued ruffian, but I bumped into another man, causing the ale to slosh from his bowl. He took a swing at me, cursing; I ducked into the throng.

Why hadn't the doctor returned? He had said *forthwith*. How long had it been?

I began to make my way toward the stairs where last I'd seen him. I edged between the seamen, trying not to get shoved or stepped on, scanning the room as I went. When I had nearly reached the stairs, I caught sight of a familiar face.

Hauk.

He had come back.

And the other one too—the skinny one with the lantern.

Hauk was bound for London, I recalled, so I might have to face him in time . . . but not now.

I slipped into the stairwell and started climbing. It was narrow and dark here, the steps steep and rough, with no railing to hang on to. Halfway up, I turned to look behind me.

Nobody following. Good.

The stairs ended at a landing on the second floor. I peered down the long, dim hallway toward the flickering glow at the farthest door, which stood a little way ajar. Voices inside; two men seemed to be arguing. And one of the voices was the doctor's.

I tiptoed partway down the hall to hear better.

"I can't ask him to do that!" the doctor said.

"Why not? If he takes food from the mouths of my working sailors, he's got to earn it. And I need proof—not just some crackbrained hunch of yours."

"He won't do it, Rolf. We'll lose him."

"We'll just *take* him, then. Easy enough."

"It doesn't work like that. If he's forced, he'll be no good to us. He'll vex the bear, not calm her."

"Pah! He's desperate. A runaway, you said, without a penny to his name. Besides, someone's got to buckle that harness. The trapper said . . ." The voice dimmed to a low growl that I couldn't quite understand.

I crept nearer, until I was right outside the door. My heart was pounding in my throat, in my ears— pounding out, *run, run, run*. But I had to hear.

". . . could maul him," the doctor was saying.

"And if that befalls, we'll know the boy's no use to us."

"If she mauls him, he'll be no use to anybody ever again."

I didn't like the sound of this. I turned to leave, but my toe banged into something hard—a chamber pot—which went clattering down the hall, spewing its foul contents along the floorboards. A commanding voice called out, "Who goes there?"

I ran. Heavy footsteps sounded behind me. I might have escaped if I hadn't slipped in the trail of filth left by the treacherous pot. A hand caught my cloak at the scruff of my neck and stopped me cold. "What's your business here, you little scoundrel?"

"Ah, Arthur, there you are." The doctor's voice this time. The hand spun me round, and I saw the doctor standing in the doorway. "I see you've met the captain," he said. "Come along within, lad, and we'll talk."

CHAPTER 8

Wolf's Den and Rathole

I HAD NO choice, for the captain shoved me down the hallway before him and into the room, bolting the door behind us. He glared at me all down the blade of his long, crooked nose—his eyes, frost blue and piercing, overhung by a thornbush of pale and wiry brows. Behind him, I could make out a narrow bed and a fireplace with a sputtering flame.

"Well?" the captain demanded.

I didn't know what he meant for me to say. Did he want me to tell what I'd been doing in the hallway? Or to explain, someway, about the bear?

The captain hoisted an unruly brow and then

turned to the doctor. "He doesn't look like much," he said. "Does he speak?"

"Arthur," the doctor said. "The captain wants to see for himself how it is with you and the bear before he agrees to grant you passage. We'll return to the warehouse, and—"

"So she can maul me? So I'll be no use to anybody ever again?"

"You little weasel!" the captain said. "I'll maul you myself, never mind the wretched bear."

The doctor held up a pacifying hand. "Nobody wants you mauled, Arthur. I told you—you won't have to go in the cage, just near it."

The captain made a scornful grunting noise; the doctor shot him a look.

"But if you show us that you can help to calm the bear," the doctor went on, "we'll grant you passage to London. What say you?"

"*I* say, why give him a choice?" the captain growled. "Let's just haul him in there and—"

"Because that won't serve us." The doctor's voice had risen. "Never mind the harness! I can't get near enough to use it anyway. Don't you see? The bear isn't eating; she isn't sleeping; she paces night and day. The skin on her flanks is festering, and she comes after me every time I try to treat her. We can't have her looking diseased when we deliver her, or worse yet, dying on us. I've told you before—"

"At length," the captain said. I could hear the grate of irony in his voice. "But I tell you—"

"She'll spook the crew—you know it! If the boy can calm her, it'll go better for all of us."

"I told you I'm for it, Garth. Let's take him in there and see what happens."

"Outside the cage. With his consent. If we force him against his will, the bear'll sense it in him— Don't argue with me; I know this bear; she *will*—and that'll put everyone at risk."

The captain cocked a bushy eyebrow. "Put *you* at risk," he said. "The bear is in your charge. Your neck is on the line."

"If something goes wrong, don't think the king won't take it out of your hide too."

I stared at him. The king?

I serve a very powerful man.

The king? This was the king's bear?

The captain crossed his arms over his chest and leveled a flinty eye at me. "Well, say something, won't you? Useless boy," he grumbled.

"Make up your mind, Rolf," the doctor said. "One

moment he's useless; the next you're sending the press-gang for him."

"You dare talk to me that way?"

"Until we're aboard ship, I do." But the doctor took in a deep breath and went on more mildly. "Captain, this serves all three of us. For you and me, it's smooth passage for the bear. For Arthur, it's a way to London."

London. At once, something dawned on me. The doctor had said: *A gift. From one very powerful man to another.*

"So," I said, "this bear is a gift from King Haakon to . . . the king of England? To King Henry?"

"You told him?" the captain sputtered. "Now the word'll be out to every guttersnipe and spy in Bergen."

"I didn't, but there's no call to keep it secret," the doctor said. "Henry's expecting it. What matter who else knows?"

"Lord save me from fools! If you've let out that there's a royal gift aboard my ship, the pirates'll come swarming at us from every wolf's den and rathole."

The doctor sighed, but I was still fixed on King Henry. My father had fought with Prince David of Wales against Henry. But David was dead, and his nephews had made peace with England, and so Henry would have no bone to pick, even with the son of a former enemy. Would he?

"What say you, Arthur?" the doctor asked. "Let's visit the bear again. I pledge my word that you'll be safe. You won't have to set a toe within the cage. And," he added, "you'll be doing a service for King Haakon. If something's amiss with the bear, it will reflect badly on the king and on Norway."

Let the king get someone else to help, I thought, for I had a bad feeling about this bear. Likely it had been a fluke with her before . . . though I had sensed something, some odd communion between us. But clearly these men weren't going to protect me. Well, the doctor might try, but the captain outranked him, and in any case, the doctor was looking to spare his own neck.

And how would I get to Wales? It was a long way from London, and I had no coin for lodging or provisions . . .

"You would take me to Wales?" I asked. "To my kin there?"

The captain rolled his eyes, but the doctor said, "Yes. If you show us that you can calm the ice bear, I'll guarantee you passage to Wales."

They were looking at me now. Waiting. The fire

suddenly popped and flared, and shadows played across their faces, making them look sinister in one moment, benign in the next.

To reclaim my birthright, my lands. To train the royal horses and ride with the princes, like my father before me . . .

"Very well," I said.

≣ CHAPTER 9 ≣

Soft Nose Whisper

BEFORE WE SAW the bear, we heard her—a heavy, rhythmic tread, a thump, a clang. Beyond the reek of fish, I sniffed out the feral musk of her.

We crept through the dark warehouse—the doctor, the captain, and I—until I made out a large, pale, moving form in the deep gloom ahead. The doctor motioned us to stop, and we watched from behind a stack of crates and bales. This bear was as tall as a pony, longer than a caribou, and as wide as two bulls. Back and forth she paced in her cage, and back and forth again, her head swinging side to side on her long neck, the convex bow of her snout lending her an air of nobility. The bear-smell now filled the air, and the stench of dung as well. A surge of fear rose up in me, turning my bones and sinews to liquid.

I would not have to go inside the cage, I told myself. The doctor had pledged it. And they needed me.

The bear paced in a shuffling, pigeon-toed gait, her front legs wide and shaggy. At each end of her cage, she tossed and rolled her head, with an impatient chuffing sound.

"Only go near," the doctor said softly. "Not near enough to be in danger, but—"

"But near enough that we can see *something*," the captain grumbled. "We didn't come here to watch you cower behind the hardtack and cod."

I felt a dark, cold place open up within me. I had said that I would do it, but now I didn't want to. To tell the truth, I was thinking that I had fled from home in foolish haste. My legs itched to run, to take me back, back to the steading, where the most fearsome creatures I was likely to encounter were Baldur and Loki; and the sober, gentle horses; and the sheep.

I glanced back toward the warehouse door, wondering if I could just drop the lantern and flee. But now the doctor was taking the lantern from me. He was saying, "Arthur, think of your father's family; think of Wales."

He was saying, "We need your help, Arthur. I wouldn't ask you to do anything that would harm you."

But would he? I didn't know this man. And even if he didn't put me in danger now, what proof did I have that he wouldn't later, when we were at sea, with nowhere to run?

The bear let out a sound, long and low. You could call it a growl, perhaps, though not a roar. You could call it a grunt or a groan. But there was something sad about it, something pathetic and mournful.

I swallowed, moved toward the sound.

When I was within the length of a man's body to the bear, she turned and faced me, her great black nose searching, searching. I could see the unbuckled harness dangling off to one side of her. She made the sound again, and then, seeming to see me at last, stood absolutely still except for her sniffing nose. But I could feel the hum that was pent up within her, something that wanted to run.

I know how it is, I thought. I know how you feel.

I edged close to her. The humming was strong within me. The bear moved her nose between the bars and began to snuffle at me.

"Arthur . . . ," the doctor said in a warning voice from behind.

The captain huffed out a sigh.

I edged nearer still—near enough to smell the ripe bear-breath, almost near enough for the searching, reaching nose to find me. Maybe the bear smelled the drippings of the rabbit haunch I had given her, or maybe she smelled the venison I had recently eaten, or maybe she smelled the running on me. Or maybe she heard me humming.

Humming. Aloud now, I realized. Not just in my head. I leaned in, between two iron bars, and the bear sniffed the air all about my face and breathed me in, breathed in the song I hummed.

"Arthur!" I felt the doctor pluck at my cloak and try to pull me back, but I broke away and, still humming, moved my face in close to the bear.

I felt the soft nose whisper across my brow, my cheeks, my mouth. I could see that the collar part of the harness was fastened securely, but the part that spanned the bear's back hung unattached. Slowly, I put my arms between the bars and groped for the loose ends and buckles of the harness, the parts meant to fasten across her chest. My fingers found them, discovered the ins and outs of them. Slowly, clumsily, I buckled the ends together. I hesitated, then shyly stroked the bear's fur along the side of her neck. It felt coarse and thick.

She made a small sound that started out rumbly and rose up into a sort of question. You might call it a grunt. You might call it a greeting. Then she turned away from me and sprawled out on the cage floor. She laid down her head and, with a great, weary moan, closed her eyes. But one of her back feet, the size of a tomcat, reached toward the bars near me and pressed itself against the toe of my boot.

I hummed. The pressure of the bear's foot against my boot felt warm and alive. In a moment, though, the humming went out of me. I breathed in and out a few times in silence, then backed my head from between the bars and turned round to face the two men.

The doctor pulled me away from the cage. "How did you know to do that?" he murmured. "To hum?"

I shrugged. "I don't know. It happened."

"So," the doctor said. His hands moved to rub his eyes; suddenly, he looked weary. He turned to the captain. "Well?"

The captain knit his tangled brows and regarded me appraisingly with those eyes of his. His gaze moved past me, to the bear. He shrugged. "God only knows what that creature will do in heavy seas. God only knows if the boy will be able to soothe it then. But if you think he might be of use, I'm willing to take him aboard."

CHAPTER 10

The *Queen Margrete*

THE CAPTAIN WAS right about one thing: every guttersnipe in Bergen seemed to have turned out the next morning to watch the king's bear being loaded onto a ship. Somehow, the word had spread. And not only guttersnipes—grown men of every description swarmed the docks as well. Fishermen and sailors, merchants and beggars, carpenters and smiths. Some women were there too: fishwives, serving maids, mothers with babes in arms. Children darted in and out among the rabble, and all seemed in a festive mood— laughing, singing, shouting.

I stuck close behind the doctor as he threaded his

way through the throng on the quay. At last he halted and pointed at the ship before us. "There she is," he said. "The *Queen Margrete.*"

She was a large vessel, and though broad abeam, far more beautiful than the chunky foreign cogs that squatted at the docks. She had a straight sternpost and rudder, like the newer ships, with a sterncastle built onto the post. But her prow swept up into a fluid Norse curve, graceful and proud.

Seamen scrambled to and fro, hefting crates and bales up the gangplank. The captain called out orders, and a great, tall crane was wheeled onto the quay. And now, through the din of the mob, I heard a chuffing sound from somewhere behind us.

The bear.

I couldn't see her over the heads of the folk, but I heard the change in their voices—a long, drawn-out *ooh.* I sensed a shifting movement in the crowd, and soon I heard the creaking wheels of a cart. And then there she was—the bear—pacing back and forth in her cage.

She was magnificent—her long, patrician snout lending her a dignified mien; her fur a tawny hue somewhere between white and gold.

I half feared that the doctor would tell me to go to

her and try to calm her, but he put a hand on my shoulder and said, "Wait."

Now, one of the seamen was climbing up onto the cart, to the top of the cage. He made a comical show of cringing before the bear below him; the crowd roared. The captain gestured at him and shouted angrily, but his words were swallowed in the din. Dangling a chain with a stout iron hook, the arm of the crane swung out over the cage. The seaman on top fastened the hook to one of the bars and jumped back down onto the quay.

With a creaking of rope, the bear's cage began to lift and turn. The bear bawled in protest; the cage rocked, and the bear slid from one end to another, scrambling for purchase on the teetering floor, thumping hard against the bars. The crowd shouted with laughter.

"Fools!" the doctor muttered. "She's a living creature, not a tun of ale."

I held my breath as the crane's arm slowly pivoted above the quay, and the cage came to hover above the ship. A shout—the captain—and the cage, swaying back and forth, began its slow descent toward the deck of the *Queen Margrete*. A sudden *crack*; a hiss of rope. The cage hurtled down and hit with a crash.

I made for the ship, but the doctor caught my arm. "Arthur, wait," he said. I twisted out of his grasp, pushed through the throng, and ran across the gang-plank. Ahead, through the bars, I could see the bear. She was huddled in a corner. Completely silent and still.

I jumped onto the deck and ran to her. The cage had fallen a little way astern of the mast; it was squashed on one end and out of kilter overall. The bear did not move.

"Boy!" the captain shouted. I turned round to see a row of faces peering at us from the quay—the captain and the doctor among them.

The captain drew his bushy brows together. "Well, see to her, boy," he said. "Is she alive?"

I made myself go still and watched the bear closely. Yes. I could see a slight breath rise in her back and sides.

Alive.

I moved to the corner where she lay and crouched beside her. We sat there together, breathing. I began to hum.

The bear groaned. She shifted her body someway and turned her head toward me. She gave a hoarse little roar, right into my face—a faint echo of her earlier roars, as if to tell me she was still not happy with what had befallen. She clambered to her feet and began to sniff about the edges of her cage, walking with that pigeon-toed shuffle and nary a limp about her.

A cheer went up from the men. The bear ignored it. The captain called out to me, "Inspect the cage, boy. Make sure she can't escape." I did, noting that one corner of the cage had splintered some deck planking and that a few of the bars had bent a little, though not so far as to leave a bear-sized gap. I tugged at every bar, and none came loose. The door, though, no longer fit rightly—it was latched, but hung askew. The entire cage had gone a bit awry, and one of the hinges had twisted.

When I told the captain what I had seen, he sent two sailors to repair the hinge while I stayed near the bear to calm her. After they had done, the captain called to me, "Move your feet, boy, what are you waiting for? The men have real work to do, and you're standing in our way."

They came pouring across the gangplank, then, a wave of racket and turmoil. I found a quiet spot near the prow and stood watching, wondering if there had been a single day in my life before now when I had run toward trouble rather than away.

PART II

THE NORTH SEA

CHAPTER 11

Dung

AND SO WE set sail on a clear and breezy morning in early June. The great, square, red-and-gold–striped shroud bellied out before us, and men scampered up and down the ratlines, calling out to one another and singing as they worked. The wind tugged at my hair and clothing, and the salt air cleared my head, and a hopeful, buoyant feeling arose within me—the kind of feeling you have when you are off on a great adventure, and the world feels large and full of possibility, and it seems as if even the ill-favored stepson of a farmer might sail into another realm entirely, riding into battle as the trusted companion of princes.

I paced the deck, jumping out of the seamen's way from time to time and watching them at their work with not a small bit of envy, for I knew I wasn't one of them; I was still only a boy-man, still only the keeper of the bear.

Which soon became all too clear.

"Boy!"

A seaman, solid as a barrel and shaped just the same, strode toward me across the deck. His face was deeply tanned and creased with many wrinkles, and a braided pigtail, streaked with gray, hung down his back. He thrust a long-handled hoe at me, and then a pail, and then he pointed in the direction of the bear cage. "It's time to earn your keep."

※

It was the loose kind, the kind that jiggles in a heap, like meat jelly cooling on a platter. Like a dozen good-sized meat jellies, all massed in a steaming mound. It was different from horse dung or sheep dung, which I had cleaned up many times before. This was bigger. Blacker. Wetter. Worse still, when the ship rolled, the mound shuddered and swayed, then crept along the floor of the bear's cage like a giant mollusk, leaving a wide, brown, slimy trail behind.

It reeked. I breathed through my mouth to mute

the smell of it, but it burned my throat and stung my eyes. I glanced at the bear, who was sprawled in the far corner of her cage in an attitude of sleeping, and yet one eye remained open and seemed to be watching me. I gripped the hoe's handle and thrust it between the iron bars, reaching for the mound of dung.

The ship pitched. I grabbed for one of the bars to keep from falling. The mound lurched away from me and zigzagged across the cage floor, now well out of reach of my hoe.

"Would you hurry up with that?" one of the seamen yelled. "It stinks to high heaven!"

I found my balance, gripped the hoe in one hand and the pail in another, and edged round the cage, closer to where the dung had settled. I set down the pail, poked the hoe between the bars, and reached for the mound. I nearly had it, until the ship rocked again. I hacked off a chunk of dung and held it in place, but another chunk—the larger one, nine or ten meat jellies' worth—skidded off in yet a different direction.

I drew in the captured bit and pulled it between the bars. I turned round to fetch the pail, but it had rolled away from me. I reached for it, dropping the hoe. The ship lurched again; I flung out my arms for balance, stepping into the pile of captive dung. My feet slipped out from under me; I hit down on one hip, splattering dung across the deck.

A laugh erupted from the seamen near the bow. "Clumsy oaf," someone said. The voice was familiar. I looked up and laid eyes on him:

Hauk.

"Filthy!" someone else chimed in.

"You're stinking up the place."

"Get moving, Dung Boy." Hauk, again.

"Dung Boy!" This from the skinny sailor I'd seen earlier with Hauk, the one named Ottar.

I felt heat rise in my face; suddenly, I was warm all over. I took hold of one of the cage bars and hauled myself to my feet. The last mound of dung was slithering away from me. Quickly, before it could escape, I went after it with the hoe. The dung dodged once, dodged twice, but I was on to its tricks now, and with a mighty thrust of the hoe, I trapped it.

Got you!

I was dragging it back toward the pail when the bear, in her corner, yawned, clambered to her feet, and began to piss. Across the floor of the cage came a gushing, foul-smelling torrent. It spurted up the side of the dung heap, submerged it, ran rolling across the deck, and lapped over the toes of my boots.

Laughter roared.

"Dung Boy!"

"I hate you, Bear," I muttered. "I hate you, I hate you, I hate you."

≩ CHAPTER 12 ≩

Not Like Horses

LATER, AFTER I had scraped the cage floor clean
and rinsed it with buckets of salt water; after I had
swabbed the soiled part of the deck, hauled up a
basketful of fish from the hold, and tossed them one
by one into the cage for the bear; after I had rubbed
off the muck from my cloak and tunic, rinsed out my
stockings, and scraped and stowed my boots, decid-
ing to go barefoot like most of the crew . . . After all
of that, the old seaman who had told me to earn my
keep appeared beside me, told me to fetch my spoon
from the storeroom, and led me to the prow, where
a man was setting out hardtack biscuits and wooden

bowls of cod stew. The second man greeted the older one by name—Thorvald—and handed him a bowl, which Thorvald passed along to me. "Eat hearty," he said, then took a bowl for himself and squatted down among a half dozen younger sailors sitting cross-legged on the deck nearby.

Hauk peered up at me with the unfriendly smile I knew well, a smile my stepbrothers often gave me when they were ranged against me and I had no hope. "Dung Boy," he muttered, and a couple of others snorted.

Thorvald skewered them all with a hard, sweeping glance; they turned away and took to their various pursuits—some tucking into their meals, a few playing cards or dice, and one of them—Hauk's minion, the thin Ottar—whittling a stick of wood.

I took my spoon and ate. Soon, talk rose around me—gossip—mostly about men I didn't know. But when the topic veered to the doctor, I pricked up my ears. He had formerly been King Haakon's physician, they said, but he had botched a minor surgery on the king's favorite niece, leaving her face badly scarred. The king had been enraged. He had dismissed the doctor from his service and, as further punishment, assigned him to tend to the bear on its way to London.

If the bear arrived sick or injured, well, there were many theories as to what would befall the doctor, but all agreed that the penalty would be dire.

Somebody called for Thorvald, who clambered stiffly to his feet and set off toward the captain's quarters in the sterncastle.

"Dung Boy." Hauk, again.

Snickers.

A copper-haired seaman said, "Hauk, that was *your* duty when we had horses aboard, but nobody called you names for it."

"I just cleaned it up, Ketil; I didn't chase it."

Ottar looked up from his whittling and guffawed.

"Well," Ketil said, "it's not like horses, is it? Mind what that beast did to the doctor. I saw his arm right after. Sliced clear to the bone, it was."

The others grew suddenly sober. One man crossed himself; another muttered and shook his head.

"Just the same," Hauk said, "he stole my supper last night, and so now . . ."

He lunged at my bowl and speared my last hunk of cod with his knife.

Staring directly into my face, he took a bite and chewed with obvious relish.

Out of the corner of my eye I caught a flickering

of glances. Ottar let out an uneasy snicker; the rest looked down and away.

I knew I ought to fight to get my dinner back. But Hauk was bigger and stronger, and right now, I was too heart-weary to try.

CHAPTER 13

These Selfsame Stars

THAT NIGHT, I wrapped myself up in the sheepskin bedroll Thorvald had given me and curled up on the deck among some of the other seamen, listening to the unfamiliar sounds. The constant swish of the sea. The creak of the mast, the snap and whisper of the sail. The muffled thuds and scrapes of cargo shifting below.

Someone snored nearby. Someone else mumbled in his sleep. And, farther off but still unmistakable, I heard the *thump thump thump* of the pacing of the bear.

She was restless tonight.

I drew my head down within the folds of my cloak,

trying to muffle the sound, but I couldn't block out the memory of her crashing to the deck in her cage, and her hoarse little roar of complaint.

Thump. Thump. Thump.

I flung back my cloak, turned over onto my back, and gazed up at the stars, glimmering through a milky-bright wash of moonlight. All at once, I wondered if Mama was looking at these selfsame stars right now. Maybe she couldn't sleep either, tonight, wondering where I was.

Had they searched for me? Scoured the sheds, the boathouse, the caves high in the fells? Had they spread out to neighboring farms and asked to comb through their byres?

Were they sorry, now that I was gone? Did they wish they'd treated me better?

Mama . . .

Was she missing me now?

Right now?

What kind of son would leave his own dear mother without a word?

A great wave of aching engulfed me. What was I doing here? Why had I left Mama and home? Were they truly *so* bad, my stepbrothers? Though they were scornful and rough, they hadn't truly harmed me. It was just . . . hard play. It was how they were. And now I was Dung Boy—no betterment whatsoever.

Thump. Thump. Thump.

I sat up. I couldn't lie here anymore. I slung my knapsack over one shoulder, picked up my bedroll, and tiptoed around the sleeping bodies until I came to the bear in her cage.

"You can't sleep either?" I asked her. Softly, so no one could hear me talking to a bear. She swung her great head in my direction and kept on with her pacing.

I sat beside the cage and took the letter from my knapsack. In the moonlight, the ink strokes stood out clear against the parchment. I drew a finger down the page and picked out the word that Mama had recognized as my father's name: *Morcan.* Then I sought out the word she had guessed was my own: *Arthur.*

So often had Mama told me about the place where I was born that I could summon it clearly in imagination. A place between the shoulders of the mountains and the curved plane of the salt marsh that swept down to the blue gray of the sea. A place of many mists and winter rains, of pastures ringed about with rowan and oak, a place that was green all the yearlong.

I could see myself, now, standing before the high timber gate to the castle. It would creak open, and . . .

Surely the four princes, David's nephews, must recol-
lect my father. Surely they would embrace me as my
father's heir and a true son of Wales.

A soft grunt startled me. The bear, no longer pacing. She gazed at me, her black nose sniffing at the
air. I held myself perfectly still. For a long moment we
held each other's eyes. Then she let out a great, heav-
ing sigh, enveloping me in a cloud of fish-smelling
bear-breath, and lowered herself to the ground. She
pressed her head against the bars, rubbing one ear
against them, and then the other.

I folded the letter and returned it to my knapsack.
I knelt beside the cage and began to hum. I knew she
was dangerous—a wild animal—but in that moment,
she brought to mind my old dog, Loki, who often kept
me company when I was lonesome. Who loved when I
scratched behind his ears.

The bear's head was massive, nearly the size of my
chest, but her ears were rounded, furry half circles no
bigger than the palm of my hand.

I reached out my fingers.

Drew them back.

Reached them out.

Drew them back.

Reached them out.

And, still humming, let my fingers graze one of her ears.

The ear twitched. Hesitant, I stroked the fur just behind it. She pushed her head against my hand, as Loki used to do when he craved a deeper scratch. I dug my fingers all the way down to the black skin beneath the white-gold fur. The bear groaned. She turned her head and presented her other ear for me to scratch.

I scratched and hummed. Hummed and scratched. Clouds of fluff came off her and wafted into the air; she must be molting. Her body heat warmed my hand.

At last she sighed and turned away. She sprawled out flat onto her belly, splaying her legs in all directions. One foot pushed back partly through the cage bars near me, pressing against my knee.

The moon was setting now. The stars burned bright against the distant sky.

I wondered if bears ever noticed stars, or thought about them. I wondered if somewhere a young bear was gazing up at these selfsame stars and yearning for his mother.

CHAPTER 14

River of Blood

AT FIRST IT looked to be an uneventful voyage. The weather held clear; the wind, brisk. We sailed south, into the waters beyond the tip of Norway, and along the coastline of the Danish peninsula. We stopped at a couple of ports along the way to restock our food and water.

The bear soon grew accustomed to the rocking of the ship. She flexed and stretched as the deck rolled beneath our feet and often hoisted her great black nose into the air to sniff, seeming to read signs in the wind as learned men read markings on parchment. And, though she did not pace as constantly as before, I could feel a great, restless longing in her, a longing to be free and away.

As for me, I was hungry. For three days, Hauk stole the better part of my supper, leaving only bits of biscuit when it pleased him. I tried taking my bowl and eating apart from the others, but Hauk followed me. I tried stuffing the food into my mouth the moment the cook gave it to me, but Hauk slapped me on the back until I choked. I tried gulping bits of the bear's raw fish when no one was looking, but after that, my belly roiled all night.

Even worse than the hunger was the shame—how some averted their eyes from me when Hauk pinched my food or called me "Dung Boy"; how Ottar parroted Hauk's taunts; how others regarded me with silent pity. The slights and jeers of my stepbrothers reached out to me from across the waters, reminding me that, while my father had been a nobleman who rode with the prince of Wales, I myself was of no account.

On the fourth day Hauk was there at the stewpot, waiting for me. As the cook reached to give me my bowl, Hauk took it in my stead. "He's giving me *his* from now on, aren't you, Dung Boy?" The cook hesitated. He must have known that Hauk filched most of my supper, but I'd always had a chance at it before. I could feel the eyes of all the others on me.

Ottar said, "Dung Boy," and a hot gush of rage spurted up within me. I put down my head like a bull and plowed into Hauk's belly. I heard an *oof*, as he staggered backward. I laid about him with fist and foot, and felt a satisfying thump as one fist landed squarely on his ribs and then another. He crashed onto the deck, the bowl flying. I fell upon him again, kicking and swinging, but now his hand was on my face, and another hand pushed hard against my neck, and I couldn't breathe . . . And before I quite knew how it had happened, I was flat on my back with blows raining down upon every sore and smarting part of me. By the time Thorvald appeared and pulled Hauk off me, I was choking on the thick, salty flood at the back of my throat, and a river of blood was gushing down my chin.

CHAPTER 15

Another Kind of Beast

THE DOCTOR SAT back on his stool. "Well," he said, "it's not as bad as I thought."

He wrung out the bloody rag into the bucket at his feet, then hung it over the rim. He applied a stinking, stinging potion to the cut above my eye. I sat very still, cross-legged on the deck, clenching my teeth against the pain. The doctor stoppered the bottle and stowed it in his sea chest, then picked up my cap and set it back on my head. "There was a lot of blood," he said. "I feared you might need stitches, but it's a shallow cut for all that. You're young—there'll be more swelling, but you'll be good as new in a fortnight or so. Your nose has stopped bleeding, and the cuts on your lip and cheek are trifles. You'll have bruises aplenty on those ribs, but they'll heal soon enough."

So if they were all such paltry injuries—trifles!— why was it I could barely see out of one eye, and my head throbbed like thunder, and my chest felt as if it had been kicked by a horse?

The doctor took the lamp and set it back on the bracket that hung from the ceiling. He had taken me to the storeroom, one of two small, enclosed chambers beneath the sterncastle; the other was the captain's quarters. The tiller ran through a gap between the rooms, and the helmsman stood just outside. "Eat hearty," the doctor said, "and rest when you can, and—"

"How?" I demanded. "How am I supposed to eat hearty when he takes my food from me every—"

I stopped. I shouldn't have said anything. My stepbrothers had taught me well the lesson that tattling only makes it worse.

"He takes . . ." The doctor frowned. "Who? You mean Hauk?"

I shrugged.

"So, what have you been eating?"

"He leaves the biscuit sometimes," I said. "And there's the bear's fish—"

"The bear's raw fish? You're eating that?"

I shrugged again.

"Arthur, those fish aren't fit to eat! God only knows how old they are by now. Listen, I'll have words with Hauk, put a spoke in his wheel—"

"No! Don't do that!"

"I need you strong and well, Arthur. You have important work to do."

And his own neck, I recalled, was on the line.

"Don't talk to Hauk," I said. "Please."

"But you can't . . ." The doctor sighed, settled back down on the stool, and, leaning toward me, laid a hand on my shoulder.

Beyond the little room, I could hear the churning of the sea and the whuff of the wind in the sail. I could hear the creak of the tiller and the clunk of the helmsman's footsteps just outside, and the companionable grunts and calls of men working together. And now, to my horror, I felt the burn of tears welling up behind my eyes and the heave of a silent sob deep in my chest. I hadn't wept—not once—not when Hauk was pummeling me, nor when the doctor was prodding at my wounds and dosing them with stinging potions. But the weight of sympathy in the doctor's hand on my shoulder unmanned me.

I wiped my eyes and nose on my sleeve. I drew in a shaky breath. The doctor abruptly withdrew his hand. He stood and then crossed to the door, picking his way through the heaps of sleeping rolls, seabags, and wooden chests.

If I were home, I knew what I would do. I would run, run, run up into the fells. I would stay there until the sun sank low in the sky, or maybe forever. But now there was nowhere to run to. I was trapped on this ship, with Hauk and the bear, until we came to London.

The doctor opened the door; sunlight flooded in. I rose to my feet and followed him outside, past the helmsman.

"How much longer till we come to port?" I asked.

"Where? In London?"

I nodded.

"A week, maybe two. It depends upon wind and tides. And the captain has dealings in a couple of ports along the way."

"So, we'll keep on to the south, along the Danish shore . . ."

"And from there we turn west and sail hard by the coast of the Low Countries. And then it's across the channel to London."

"How far is Wales from Lon—?" I began.

"At the far, savage rim of the civilized world," boomed a voice. The captain, striding astern, came to an abrupt halt when he saw my face. "Good Lord, Garth, what's fallen out with your boy? Did the bear—?"

"Not the bear," the doctor said mildly, "but another kind of beast—the human kind."

The captain dismissed my injuries with a wave of his hand. "Wales!" he snorted. "A backwater trading post—not worth the time nor the trouble."

I wanted to protest, for I misliked hearing my native land spoken of in that way, but the captain marched to his quarters beneath the sterncastle and shut the door firmly behind.

≣ CHAPTER 16 ≣

A Rent in the Mist

THAT NIGHT, SOMETHING roused me. I opened my eyes and found myself shrouded in a chill, clammy mist that eddied about the dim lanterns like spilt milk swirling in water. The stars had vanished, as had the mast, the sail, and all but the men sleeping nearest beside me. I could hear the creak of ropes, and the murmuring of men's voices, and the swish of water against the hull. And something else—more felt than heard—the *thud, thud, thud* of the bear pacing in her cage.

Though she often paced, even at night, something about the sound of her footfalls now troubled me.

They did not have the steady back-and-forth cadence I had become accustomed to, but started and stopped, started and stopped, in a choppy, uneasy rhythm. She was chuffing, letting out those coughing, snorting breaths that told me she was unsettled.

I rubbed my bruised eye, which felt a little better than before, and the aching in my head had abated. But now I heard a deep rumbling sound, a growl.

I rose to my feet, gooseflesh prickling my arms.

Why would she be growling . . . now?

Movement caught my eye; I looked up. Through a high rent in the mist, I beheld a vision from a dream: a tall mast reaching for the gibbous moon, too near to belong to another ship, but in the wrong place altogether to be our own. It hung there, impossibly, coming closer. . . .

Crash!

The ship lurched; I was knocked down, cracking an elbow on the boards. The night exploded around me—wood splintering, men shouting, the bear roaring. Something shifted: a thunder of footfalls surged in a wave across the deck.

Thuds. Cries. The singing clash of steel against steel.

I felt a hard thump against my side; I heard a bellow

of surprise; a body toppled heavily across my legs and then rolled off me, cursing. I scrambled to my feet, but straightaway another man rammed into me and knocked me flat. This time I made for the bear cage, which would at least give me something to hang on to. Mist eddied before me, allowing veiled glimpses of the mayhem and then swaddling all in thick, white darkness. At last the bars appeared from out of the mist. I grabbed on to one, relieved . . . but something was amiss.

Creak.

Clang.

Creak.

Clang.

Through a thin patch in the fog, I saw the cage door swing open. Slam shut. Swing ajar again.

The bear stood just within the open doorway, peering out.

CHAPTER 17

Treasure

THE DOOR CLANKED shut. Creaked open again.

I should move right now. I should shut that door, and quick.

But my feet seemed to be stuck to the deck. What if the bear saw me coming? What if I didn't get to the door in time?

Would she attack me?

The bear leaned forward, her great long snout reaching and quivering, as if the air were a solid thing that she could touch, as if she could feel out its secret promises of danger and opportunity.

Just *move*, I told myself. I forced myself to set one

foot after the other in the direction of the cage door.

Clank.

Creak.

Clank.

A man loomed suddenly before me. He clutched my arm—clutched it hard—and put his face down right in front of mine. Bulbous nose. A ragged scar across one cheek. Nobody I'd seen before. "Where's the treasure?" he rasped.

"What . . . treasure?"

"The king's treasure, what else? Don't play the fool with me, boy, or I'll—" He gave me a shake, so hard my head snapped back and my teeth rattled in my head.

Something moved behind him. Something large and white.

The man turned to see what had caught my eye. The bear growled—a low, throbbing rumble that entered the base of my spine and sent waves of prickling gooseflesh all across my back.

The man let me go and stumbled backward. A flash of steel—and then the bear was upon him. The man spat out a curse; there was a spray of blood; and then his body rose into the air and seemed to hang there in the thinning fog before it plummeted to the boards and bounced with a sickening thud.

The bear was swaying back and forth. She let out a chuffing grunt that sounded part angry and part bewildered, and then she struck out across the deck. Two men rushed at her with drawn swords, but then a slash of the bear's great claws had both of them on their backs and one of them spurting blood. A swarm of arrows came buzzing through the air at her. She let out a roar; she rose up on her hind legs; she swatted at her nose. Another man attacked; a swipe of the claws laid him out flat.

All about me men hurtled across the deck away from her; I heard splashes as they hit the water.

"Arthur!"

The doctor's voice. I turned to look for him, but though the fog was surely lifting, I couldn't make him out in the throng.

"Arthur, here!"

There—not too far away, near the hatch to the hold—there he was, waving.

I ran through the din and pandemonium, dodging unsheathed cutlasses and thrusting elbows, stepping over bodies that lay buckled and broken. The bear was growling, pacing, shaking her head, sending a fine mist of blood into the air. I heard more splashes as men leaped overboard; whether pirates or our own crew, I neither knew nor cared. I reached the hatch, shinnied a little way down the ladder, and stopped at a rung just above the doctor.

"Shut the hatch, Arthur," he said.

I did.

Overhead—dim shouts and the thunder of running footsteps. Below—an ominous gurgling sound, and a powerful reek of fish and stagnant water. A lantern bloomed to life somewhere beneath my feet, and then another.

"How did she escape?" the doctor asked.

"The cage door was open. Maybe that hinge . . ."

The doctor swore. "They never did mend that right."

Presently, it grew quieter above. I climbed up a couple of rungs, opened the hatch a crack, and looked out.

The fog had thinned a bit, and in the faint moonlight I could see that the stretch of deck before me was empty.

"Pirates?" the doctor asked.

"I don't see them, sir."

"The bear?"

I lifted the hatch higher. Still no pirates—at least, none standing. There were some lumps and smears on deck, too dim to make out clearly. Nor could I find the pirate ship. Someone had reefed our sail, and a few seamen sat on the yard beam, above. The bear I saw pacing astern, staggering a little and weaving from side to side. She stopped now to swipe at the arrow that pierced her snout. Two more arrows bristled from her leg and shoulder, and one ear seemed to have been torn, and blood soaked her head and neck and chest. Slippery red tracks followed her across the deck.

"She's hurt," I said.

"How badly?"

"Three arrows. A lot of blood. But maybe not all of it's hers."

The doctor swore again.

The bear lurched toward the sterncastle, on top of which, I now saw, many of our crewmen had fled to safety. She rose to stand on her hind legs and snuffled at the parapet. The men shifted back, away from her. The bear groaned, then thumped down on all fours and turned away.

I scooted down a few rungs and pulled the hatch cover tight. My heart, beating fast, felt oddly swollen and tender in my chest.

"The pirate said 'treasure,'" I murmured.

"What?"

"That's what the pirate said to me," I said.

"Which pirate?"

"The one near the bear cage. The one the bear . . ." Well. I didn't know, exactly, what the bear had done to him. Maimed him, certainly. Maybe killed him.

"'Treasure'?"

"'King's treasure.' He asked me where it was. He . . . shook me."

It sounded childish when I said it. With all the blood, and the bear wounded, and some men likely dead . . . *He shook me.*

"The captain was right," the doctor said. "Those pirates must have heard something in port and thought we had king's treasure aboard."

"Do you think they know?" I asked. "That the bear is the treasure?"

"The bear . . . ?" By the dim lantern light, I could see the doctor's gaze sharpen. He laughed dryly, gave me a grim little smile. "I hope they do now," he said.

I heard the bear's footsteps on the deck, drawing near. I heard her halt just above. I held my breath. Could she smell me? Would she try to pry open the hatch?

Some small part of me yearned to go up there and hum to her, maybe scratch behind her ears. But the greater part wanted to stay down here, in the dark, where it was safe.

The bear's footsteps thumped again, moving away.

I sighed out a deep breath. Below, I heard the swish of water. Above, only the bear.

I would have asked the doctor *What happens now?* except that I feared what his answer would be.

≋ CHAPTER 18 ≋

Footfalls

IT WAS QUIET, save for the pacing of the bear on deck and the gurgle of water below. I looked down and saw by the swaying lantern light that water was rising in the hold. The pirate ship must have breached us. From time to time, I heard voices from the sterncastle, and, once, I heard a man's footsteps running on the deck above. My fingers began to feel cramped from clinging to the ladder, and I longed to climb up on deck and give them a rest. But whenever I closed my eyes, I saw the slash of claws and the spray of blood and the thump and bounce of the pirate's body on the boards.

Just as I was beginning to wonder if we would be forced to stay like this all night, or maybe forever, the captain's voice bellowed from above:

"Doctor!"

"Scoot down, Arthur," the doctor said. He crawled over me, cracked open the hatch, and looked about, no doubt checking for the whereabouts of the bear.

"Doctor!" the captain shouted again. Sounding vexed now.

The doctor lifted the hatch wider and turned to face the sterncastle. "Yes, sir?"

"Don't say I didn't tell you!"

"No, sir."

"I warned you about pirates."

"You were right, sir," the doctor admitted.

"Where is that rapscallion of yours, that Arthur?"

"He's here, sir. What do you want with him?"

"You know bloody well what I want with him! Why else is he taking up precious space on my ship and laying waste to my working men's rations?"

There it was. The captain cared nothing for my life, but only for his commission with the bear.

The doctor shifted his weight on the ladder and looked down at me. "Arthur, can you persuade the bear to go quietly back into her cage?"

How in heaven's name did he think I could do that?

"You want me to go up there with her?" I asked. "Alone?"

The doctor held my gaze for a moment, then turned back to the captain. "We're . . . devising a plan," he called.

To me, again, he said, "Listen. Remember how you hummed to the bear that time?"

"Yes, but—"

"For God's sake, Garth, we're breached! We don't have all bloody night!" the captain roared. "Have that do-nothing layabout of yours hitch a couple of ropes to the bear's harness, and my men will drag the blasted beast into its cage."

"She won't sit still for me to tie the ropes," I told the doctor. "She's hurt, and riled."

"Rest easy, sir, I've got a plan!" the doctor shouted. I heard him sigh, and then in a low voice he muttered to me, "I think we'll have to come at this from a couple of directions at once."

\||//

The doctor called down orders to the hold below, and presently, he and I were standing calf-deep in the frigid water at the base of the ladder. Close by stood three seamen wielding pots and spoons, another man with two red kerchiefs, and a fifth man with a string of metal pails tied together. They did not look happy.

The plan was this: The five of them would go on deck and move astern, putting the bear between them and the cage. They would shout and set up a din with their implements. One man would wave the red handkerchiefs, and together, they would drive the bear toward the cage.

"What if it won't go?" one of the men asked.

"She doesn't like loud noise—we've seen that," the doctor said. "While you're distracting her, I'll dump some fish into her cage. She'll smell it. Likely, she'll just head for her supper and you won't have to do a thing."

"But what if it doesn't?" the same man asked. "What if it comes for us?"

"And what about *him*?" another sailor demanded, pointing at me. "What's he eating up our rations for if we're the ones risking our necks?"

"Never mind him," the doctor said. "If the bear attacks, just make for the sterncastle. *Run.*"

The five sailors eyed me in a way I knew well—the way my stepbrothers looked at me when my mother took me under her wing. The thought of going up on deck with the bear drained all the lifeblood out of me and left me shaking, but some stubborn knot within me rebelled at being protected because I was too weak to stand on my own. "But what . . ." My voice quavered. I cleared my throat. "What do you want me to do?"

"If this fails," the doctor said grimly, "there'll be plenty for you to do, believe me. But I'm hoping it won't come to that."

\\\\\

This plan of the doctor's seemed frail and unpromising, but it was all I had to cling to. Why would the bear give up her freedom on account of a few pots and pans?

I could hear her pacing, above. She seemed to be ranging across the entire deck.

The five sailors mounted the ladder and, with some urging by the doctor, clambered up on deck. The doctor handed me a pail full of fish, took one for himself, and told me to scale the ladder behind him. "Wait here," he said. "Shut the hatch behind me, but open it fast when you hear me call." He thrust aside the hatch and climbed outside.

In the hold, no one spoke. Above, I could hear footsteps on deck, but I couldn't tell who was who, or what they were doing.

Clank.

My heart jumped.

Clank-clank.

That must be a pot, or a pail. I waited to hear more clanks, and shouting, but there was nothing.

Nothing but the swish of water.

But now . . .

Footsteps. Someone was running. And now, heavier thumps, coming fast.

"Arthur!"

I flung open the hatch; the doctor jumped down, slamming into me. I dropped my pail and nearly toppled off the ladder entirely, but managed to hang on with fingers and a toe. The hatch banged down just as heavy footsteps came galumphing across it.

The bear.

Above, a shout.

The doctor waited a cautious moment, then cracked the hatch open and peeked out. "Come on, don't give up yet," he muttered. "Don't—"

A scream. Many voices, shouting. A great ringing clash of metal hitting the deck.

A flurry of lighter footfalls.

Silence.

Slowly, the doctor lowered the hatch.

"What happened?" I whispered.

The doctor sighed. "They're safe, on the sterncastle."

"And the bear?"

"Still loose."

≣ CHAPTER 19 ≣

Free Forever

THE DOCTOR CALLED out to the men below. He traded places with me on the ladder, leaving me at the top. After a moment, he handed me a heavy pail of fish. He spoke to me—something about moving slowly, something about climbing the mast if I had to, something about humming—but a powerful bloodwind was sweeping through my mind, and it was hard to hear him over the roar of it.

He had pledged his word to keep me safe. That was part of the pact we had made. And it was true that he had tried to protect me, but now . . .

I lifted the hatch and peered out. The sun had

edged over the horizon, and in the pale morning light I could see the bear pacing slowly back and forth not far from the sterncastle and the bulk of the crew. Arrows still bristled from her snout, shoulder, and leg. Much of the blood on her head and shoulders had turned a crusty brown, but patches of fresh red blood streaked her nose and one ear. As I watched, she plowed into an empty cooking pot; it clattered across the deck. She halted and shook her head, seeming confused, then began pacing again.

The deck was smeared with bloody footprints and littered with abandoned seabags, blankets, pots and pans and pails. Fishing nets lay in heaps beneath the yardarm, upon which stood three or four seamen. Had they tried, and failed, to net the bear? Near the bear's cage, I now saw the pirate who had demanded I show him the king's treasure—his body still and broken-looking, lying in a pool of blood. Not far from him lay two other bodies; I saw bloody claw marks where one man's tunic had been torn.

"Arthur," the doctor said softly.

The sea lapped against the sides of the ship, making a hollow sound. I heard a repeated wooden *clunk* and realized it was the pail in my hand, knocking against the ladder.

"Arthur," the doctor said again.

"You gave your word," I said. "You said I would be safe."

I saw him flinch, but he did not reply.

So that was how it was. He would protect me so long as it suited him, and then . . .

I climbed up onto the deck.

The bear didn't seem to mark my coming, but in the crowded sterncastle, all eyes were on me. I made out the captain, standing at the fore. I waited for him to shout at me—some command or disparagement—but he said nothing, nor did anyone else. A gull cried overhead. A pail rolled across the deck and hit with a *clank* against the gunwale. The bear's feet thumped against the deck as she chuffed low in her throat and paced from port to starboard and back.

Back and forth.

Back and forth.

Back and forth.

If I was going to lead her into the cage, I would first have to get her attention. I forced myself to creep toward her, ready to run away at a moment's notice.

When I was the length of three men from the bear, she halted. She turned to face me, nose twitching.

I picked up a fish from the bucket. Held it up. I

remembered how, when I had thrown the rabbit haunch at her before, the bear had seemed offended. So now I set the fish down on the deck beside my feet.

Slowly, she began to shuffle toward me.

I backed away, not taking my eyes off her.

One step.

Two steps.

Three.

Now the bear had reached the fish. She held it down with one paw and ripped off a piece to eat.

I set down another fish. I backed away.

One step.

Two steps.

Three.

The bear shook her head, seeming fuddled. She swiped at the arrow in her snout and shook her head harder. She took a small, staggering step to one side.

I began to hum.

She turned to look at me, and her eyes cleared. She moved toward the fish. Held it down with a paw and devoured it. Raised her head, sniffed the air, and began to follow me.

I moved back again.

One step.

Two steps.

My foot hit a slippery patch; I skidded and thrust out my arms for balance, spilling fish across the deck. My other foot knocked against something solid, and then both feet slithered out from beneath me. I pitched forward onto a lumpy, knobby something. . . .

A body. I recognized him now. The man named Ketil, the copper-haired man who had stood up for me against Hauk. He lifted his head, blinked, and then his eyes rolled back, and his skull hit the deck with a *thunk*.

Was he dead?

No. I could feel him breathing beneath me, praise be to God.

A grunt. I twisted round and saw with a start that the bear had come to stand just over me, sniffing, sniffing. . . .

My lungs sucked in air and would not let go of it; every part of me went still . . . except for my right hand, which reached into the bucket and fumbled for a fish. It found one and held it aloft before the bear's great black inquiring nose. She leaned in and took the fish gently in her mouth.

All the air whooshed out of me. I rolled off the man and clambered to my feet. I snatched at the handle of the pail, sliding a little in the pool of blood, and moved backward.

One step.

Two steps.

Three.

I turned, and saw the cage just behind me. I pulled the door open and stood on the threshold, looking in.

The sun lay low in the eastern sky, hemmed in by a wall of iron bars.

I stepped away from the cage. The bear was shaking her head again. She pawed at the arrow and let out a small grunt of bewilderment and pain. Behind her the sky reached down to the sea, stretching out in every direction. A flock of birds skimmed low over the water. The horizon burned gold, lighting up a fleet of scudding clouds, like ships that could sail free forever.

All at once my chest felt too small to contain the vastness of my heart, and I didn't want to go in that cage.

But I did.

The bars crowded in upon me. The cage roof darkened the sky. Still humming, I dumped out the last of the fish near the ones the doctor had set there. I backed toward the far end of the cage.

The bear lifted her nose and seemed to search the air, as if seeking something she had lost or forgotten.

She shook her head again. Then she lumbered within and tore into another fish.

I slipped out between the bars and held the door shut. Across the deck, I saw the doctor pop up from the hatch. He sprinted to the cage and handed me a lock and a stout chain. I secured the door with the chain and snapped the lock shut.

A cheer went up. Men poured onto the deck from the hatch and the mast and the sterncastle. Some of them called out to me; a few clapped me on the shoulder as they passed.

But a dark hazy line on the horizon had caught my eye. Land. How far away? I wondered. If the bear were to escape again . . .

They say that ice bears can swim for leagues and leagues.

CHAPTER 20

Sailing or Bailing

AFTER THAT, ALL the noise of the world surged up and broke over me: the captain shouting, the thunder of running footfalls on the deck, the hiss of lines, the crack of the great sail in the wind. The ship seemed to lift a little; a breeze began to whuff in my ears and tug at my hair.

The bear wasn't eating anymore. She sprawled on her belly, legs spread out to the four directions, the arrows jutting out of her. I looked about for the doctor, for the bear was his charge too—it was his job to deliver her, whole and hale, to the English king—and he had risked *my* life to do it. I saw that some, in the swarm on deck, were placing the fallen men on pallets and bearing them aft, but I couldn't find the doctor among them. The captain was strutting about in high feather, as if he had vanquished the pirates single-handedly. But it was the bear who had done it—the bear who had saved us all.

Thorvald clapped me on the shoulder. "This way, Arthur," he said. "If you're not sailing, you're bailing."

"But the doctor—"

"He's got doctoring work to do."

"But the bear—"

"Sailing or bailing! We're breached, boy, and the hole's growing."

He led me across the blood-slick deck, past the men in the bucket brigade line, to the hatch. Some of the sailors nodded at me as I passed; others smiled and said *Arthur*. And I was surprised at what a comfort it was to hear my true name on their lips.

I turned back to look at the bear, but Thorvald said, "Bail!" And since his tone brooked no argument, I joined the crewmen on the ladder. Someone handed me a pail of bilgewater from below; I passed it up to a man on deck, who gave me an empty pail; I handed it down.

Light from the hanging lanterns in the hold

shimmered across the dark surface of the water, showing that it had risen from calf-deep to thigh-deep.
A few of the smaller casks floated, knocking against
one another, and amidst them I saw dark, furry lumps
that could only be rats. Seamen sloshed about, and I
could hear the repair crew hammering. The ship's timbers creaked, and there was a rushing sound I had not
marked earlier.

More ominously, the hold did not reek, as it had
done before. It smelled fresh, of seawater.

I passed a full pail up to the deck. An empty one
down. Another full one up. And so it went, until my
legs had gone numb and a blister the size of a bilberry
had popped up on my palm. I told myself that the bear
would be fine, that the arrows had not pierced deep
enough to be deadly, that the doctor was likely seeing
to her right now. I wondered what had befallen the
man I'd bumped into—Ketil. He had taken my part
against Hauk. I hoped—

"Arthur!"

I looked up, to find the doctor himself standing
above the hatch. "Arthur, come here!"

I felt a surge of gladness rise in me upon seeing
him, and yet . . . He had put me in danger. Had gone
against his word.

I scrambled up into the morning light.

The doctor picked up a small wooden sea chest near his feet. He tucked it under one arm and took off in the direction of the bear's cage. I followed, cutting through the upper end of the bucket brigade and weaving among men swabbing the deck, wrangling lines, and bustling about with boards and ropes and buckets of nails. Above the muted sounds of hammering in the hold, I heard the captain bellowing out orders.

"Can you sew?" the doctor called back to me.

"Sew?" I blinked.

"Yes, sew! With a needle and thread."

I had often watched my mother sew, but she had never taught me. That was women's work.

"No," I said.

"Well, it's never too late to learn."

CHAPTER 21

The Arrow

THE BEAR LAY on her side, her forelegs bound together with rope, her rear legs likewise fettered. A third rope led from her harness to a bar at the rear of her cage, to which it was fastened with a good, tight knot. Her eyes were closed and, by the slow way her great, pale sides rose with her breath, I could tell that she was alive.

"How did you—?"

"I put sleeping herbs in the fish we gave her." The doctor set down his wooden chest, opened it, fetched out a ring of keys, and opened the lock to the chain that secured the cage door.

"You said you tried to stupefy her with herbs before, but to no effect."

"I used more this time. I feared making her sick, but I had no choice."

The doctor unwound the chain, picked up his chest, and followed me into the cage. "Keep your wits about you, Arthur. She might wake at any moment."

While the doctor rummaged in his chest, I drew near to the bear. A healing plaster encrusted her snout, where the arrow used to be. Another plaster covered one ear. The arrow in the bear's leg seemed to have vanished without a trace, but a broken-off wooden shaft still jutted from her left shoulder. The doctor had shorn off the fur at the base of the shaft, revealing a patch of black skin.

The bear's fur looked completely gold now, not white, as if she had absorbed the light of the morning sun. And she seemed so harmless, lying there. Like a big old sheepdog, settled down for an early nap.

"There's the trouble," the doctor said, pointing to the shaft. "The others weren't firmly lodged, but that one thrust deep. It'll fester if we don't remove it." He handed me a skein of thread and a long needle. "Thread this for me, would you?" he said. "Give me a length as long as your forearm and double it. Cut it with one of the knives in there"—he nodded at the chest—"and tie a knot at the end, son, while you're at it."

Son. The word hit me in a soft place; it burrowed in and lodged there. My stepfather had never once called me *son.*

But I told myself it was only a word. The doctor had ordered me to go on deck alone with the bear. I could have been killed. A man wouldn't do that to his son.

The hole in the needle was small, and the end of the thread kept coming unraveled. Thrice, after I had licked and twisted the thread and aimed it into the hole, the ship rocked, and the thread lurched off in the wrong direction. Still, it wasn't long before I coaxed the twisted tip through the opening. I stuck the needle into a fold in my cloak and fumbled with the ends of the thread, trying to make a knot.

"Here," the doctor said. He took the needle from me and slid his fingers down the thread to the ends. He made a quick, deft movement—not even looking at the thread—and a knot appeared. "Do you see how it's done?"

I shook my head.

"Well, another time. Hold it for now," he said, handing the needle back to me. He took the knife from his sea chest. "Stand back, Arthur." The doctor set the blade on the black skin near the arrow and pressed. The bear twitched; the doctor braced himself, as if to bolt; blood oozed out of a new cut. The bear groaned but did not open her eyes.

The doctor let out a breath. He wiggled the shaft a little. The arrow didn't budge. He wiped his brow, then set the knife edge on the bear's skin on the other side of the shaft. The blade hesitated on the surface, making a small hollow in the black skin. The doctor pushed hard, plunging it in. Blood bubbled out of the gash, seeping across the black shaved patch of skin and into the long, pale fur.

I wanted to run but couldn't look away.

"Get me a cloth from the chest."

I did. The doctor blotted the blood, then jiggled the shaft again. Something seemed to have loosened under the skin; now the shaft moved more freely. Gently, the doctor pulled, and at last the arrowhead emerged— one corner, another corner, the tip. The doctor set it down. With both hands, he pinched the edges of the bloody slit together.

"Needle," he said, and when I hesitated, "Give me the needle! Quick!"

He took it from my fingers and thrust it down

through the bear's skin on one edge of the wound, then pulled it up through another flap of skin on the other side. But the knot didn't hold.

The doctor swore.

"Make another knot in the thread on top of the first one."

I grasped the needle and fumbled to tie a second knot—painstakingly, strand by strand. I handed it back.

This time, it held.

"Blot this for me, would you?"

I sopped up blood with the cloth as the doctor went on stitching. In a moment, though, he stopped, closing his eyes. He muttered something under his breath.

"What did you say?"

"I said, take the needle."

But that wasn't what he had said. I was almost certain I'd heard it. He'd said, "I can't see."

The doctor wasn't blind—I knew that. He could tend to wounds. He could make his way down narrow alleys and through the chaos on a ship.

But he had wanted me to thread the needle. And I remembered hearing of the botched surgery on King Haakon's favorite niece.

Could the doctor not see well up close?

Maybe not.

And now he wanted *me* to do this?

"I can't sew," I said. "I told you—"

The bear groaned; her back paws twitched.

"She's rousing," the doctor said. He held out the needle. "No time to spare. Take it!"

I did.

He told me to cut the thread and pull out the last stitch, which had created a lopsided pucker in the bear's skin. He took the needle from me, knotted the thread twice, and handed it back. He told me to push the needle in on one side and poke it up through the flesh on the other, and then pull the thread so that the sides of the slit came together.

My head and eyes knew what to do—but my fingers did not. They were clumsy, clumsy. The doctor wiped away blood so I could see what I was doing, but even so, the work was maddeningly slow.

Still, the sides of the gash had begun to come together. My stitches were not even, but they looked straighter than the doctor's, and the wound was smooth, not puckered.

The bear twitched again, let out an explosive whuff. "Hurry!" the doctor said.

I reached the end of the slit and pulled out the

needle. The doctor cut the thread; I tied it. The bear shifted, kicked at her fetters. A low growl rumbled through her. Her eyes blinked open.

Blinked shut.

"Cut the ropes!" the doctor said. He handed me a knife; I sawed through the rope that bound the bear's rear legs while the doctor did the same for her forelegs. I slipped between the bars and hacked through the rope attached to the bear's harness while the doctor gathered up his wooden chest and ran for the cage door. It clanged shut just as the bear staggered to her feet.

She blinked. Shook her head. Her nose reached out—twitching, twitching—seeming to search the air for clues to what had befallen her. One paw swiped at her snout, and then her other legs slid out from under her; she landed on her belly with an *oof*. She let out a halfhearted roar, then scrambled to her feet again and began, unsteadily, to pace.

CHAPTER 22

Sleep

I COULDN'T SLEEP that night.

The events of the day crowded into my mind, unsettling me. The jolting crash when the other ship rammed us. The body lifting into the air. The captain strutting across the deck, as if *he* had vanquished the pirates. The bear shaking her head in pain and confusion; the fine spray of blood coming off her as she stumbled across the deck toward her cage. The men nodding, smiling, calling me by name. The doctor squinting down at his mangled stitches. The dead-meat feel of the needle piercing flesh. *Son.*

It was a dangerous word, a word I craved to hear,

and yet . . . Men used it carelessly. They used it to mean merely *boy*.

But the sound of the word itself—*son*—could echo down through your memories; it could quicken old longings; it could betray you.

The deck pressed hard against my hip; I turned onto my other side.

The copper-haired man—Ketil. I should have asked the doctor how he fared. Was it a pirate who had felled him? Or the bear? Would he survive?

I could hear some men still bailing. Although they had patched the breach as well as they might while still at sea, I could feel that something wasn't right. The ship lumbered heavily through the waves. Spray shot up in great, gushing fountains and pelted the deck, though the wind blew light and the seas ran smooth.

All at once, I remembered my knapsack. I'd had it with me before the pirate ship rammed us. But now . . . Where was it?

The letter.

I needed it to help me find my father's kin. For surely there would be clues written therein—names and places. I needed it as a token to prove I was my father's son.

I hadn't marked my knapsack on deck when I was alone there with the bear, though I might well have missed it. Likely, someone had returned it to the storeroom.

Tomorrow, I would search there.

I tried again to sleep, but the familiar restlessness was twitching in my legs now, was singing in my bones. I arose, taking my bedroll with me, and padded across the deck to the cage.

The bear lay sprawled on her belly, her fur frosted blue with moonlight. Her back and sides rose and fell in a slow, even rhythm.

Sleep.

The plasters on her ear and snout had nearly crumbled off; underneath, her fur was dark with dried blood. I could see the black swatch of shaven skin where I had stitched, but couldn't make out the stitches themselves to see if they yet held.

She had not touched the new fish I'd put out for her.

I squatted on my heels and watched. The bear shifted, twitched her good ear.

I leaned back, gazed up at the sky. The clouds had cleared, and the stars gleamed, dense and bright, for as far as I could see.

Somewhere, to the far north and east, the bear had been free. Maybe she had had cubs, or a mate. And now she was alone, among strangers.

As was I.

The bear shifted again. Swiped at her nose. Moaned softly.

I stood. Breathed in the night air, tinged with salt and fish. I slipped between the bars.

I did not approach the bear, but stood watching her from a far corner.

Breathe in: the great back rose.

Breathe out: it sank again.

Beneath the sounds of bailing and the hiss of the sea, I heard, or maybe just felt, a deep rumbling from the bear—a sound like a heartbeat, or like the coursing of blood, or like the deep solemn echo of stars wheeling their slow circuits across the sky.

Breathe in.

Breathe out.

Breathe in.

The round moon was striped with iron, as if the sky itself were held prisoner.

I eased myself down to the cage floor, in the corner. I leaned back against the bars. Just for a moment, I closed my eyes.

Sometime later, I looked up to find the bear's eyes open and watching me. I was not afraid.

Breathe in.

Breathe out.

Breathe in.

The bear held my gaze for a long, still time. I wondered: Am I dreaming this? Am I dreaming right now?

Then the bear yawned, showing the great, white blades of her teeth, and settled back down, tucking her eyes beneath a paw.

I slept.

CHAPTER 23

Sinister, Soft Sound

I AWOKE WITH a prickling sensation, as if some sinister, soft sound had roused me, but I didn't know what it was. I opened my eyes to swirling mists in the twilight just before dawn.

The creak of lines. The whuff of wind in the sail. The swish and thud of men bailing. Cold iron bars against my back . . .

I remembered now. The cage.

Had I been here all night?

The bear . . .

My eyes found her nearby. Asleep.

But wait. She hadn't been *there* before. She had moved in the night.

Did she know I was here, in her cage?

Whispers:

"He's waking."

"Let me do it now."

"No. You take the spoon."

"Please? You never let me—"

And then I heard it again, the sound that had awakened me. The clink of metal on metal just behind me.

I leaped to my feet.

It was Hauk—tapping one of the bars with a knife blade. *My* knife. And there was Ottar too, tapping at a different bar with . . .

My spoon case.

"Hey!" I lunged for it. Ottar jerked it back.

"Lost something, Dung Boy?" Hauk said. He held up my knapsack and dangled it before me.

The bear shifted, raised her head. I squeezed between the bars and reached for Hauk's arm, but he twisted away. "Listen," I pleaded, "you can have my spoon, but give me back the letter."

"Aww, Dung Boy wants his letter," Hauk said.

"Poor Dung Boy," Ottar said.

Hauk shoved Ottar into me; we went down together, with Ottar on top. In a moment, I was on top of *him*, raising my fist to cuff him hard. He cried

out and covered his head with his arms. I checked my
punch and flung myself at Hauk, tackling him about
the knees. He let out an *oof* as he crashed backward
onto the deck. I smote him hard, and then again, but
he was flailing at me with my knife. I rolled off Hauk
and was about to rise, when Thorvald appeared before
us. He seized Hauk's wrist, stripping the knife from
him, and then took my cloak in his fist and hauled me
to my feet.

"Enough!" Thorvald said. "Get you to work." With
a clattering of footsteps, Hauk and Ottar disappeared
into the fog. I looked about for my knapsack, but it
had disappeared too.

I picked up my cap and, when I stood, saw that
Thorvald was holding out my knife. "This is yours?"
he asked.

I nodded, took it, tucked it into my belt. I started
to leave, but Thorvald said, "Arthur, wait. What happened here?"

I opened my mouth to tell, then shut it. I didn't
want to tattle. But still, the letter . . . I *needed* it.

"Well?"

"I've . . . lost a letter," I said. "A letter addressed to
my mother."

"And Hauk took it?"

I shrugged. "He may know where it is."

"And Ottar? He's in this too?"

Ottar. He was a sniveling little ferret, but still . . . Hauk had his claws well into him. And I knew what it was to be the weak one.

"No," I said. "He had nothing to do with it."

CHAPTER 24

Listing to Starboard

THE SHIP WAS listing to starboard. Just slightly—
not so much as you'd notice—until you went below
and marked the slant of the bilgewater against the hull.
It seemed to me that the water had crept higher, too.

A low mood had settled over the ship that morning
and soured the sailors' words. Just the day before, they
had clapped me on the back while singing of victory
over the pirates. But now, as I braced myself on the
ladder and set to bailing, I merited hardly a glance,
not even from Ottar, who was bailing some few rungs
below me. Hauk, I had heard, had been assigned to the
lowest and foulest part of the bilge—as punishment for

theft, it was rumored. So, Thorvald must have taken my part against him.

"If Captain had made for land straightaway," one man grumbled, "we'd be safe and dry by now."

Another man snorted. "'No one to help with repairs ashore,' he says. 'We can repair her well enough to carry us to Bruges,' he says, 'but not so far as London.'"

"Bruges is too far! We need dry dock to fix her," the first man said, "and soon."

"And what of the pirates?" a third man put in. "We can't bail and fight at the same time. What if they come back?"

"Who's going to help with repairs when we fetch up at the bottom of the sea?" another asked.

"A school of herring?"

"A giant squid?"

"A band of mermaids?"

They joined in a burst of bitter laughter.

I handed another pail of bilgewater up the ladder. The man above me said, "So what do we do, then? Bail until our arms fall off?"

The man below me grunted, "Just pray the weather holds."

\\\\//

The stolen knapsack preyed on my mind all morning. After a time, I managed to break away from the bailing brigade and make my way to the storeroom to search for it. I left the door open the merest crack, for light . . . and nearly tripped over a body on the floor.

It was Ketil—sound asleep. The doctor must have sheltered him here.

I edged around him to the stacks of seabags and chests and began to sort through them. At last, I found my knapsack, but it was empty—no spoon, no letter.

Hauk!

Likely my things were in *his* seabag, but the bags looked nearly the same; it would take all day to go through every one. Desperate now, I rifled through the contents of some of them, to no avail.

But I did find Ottar's bag. I had seen him the night before—alone, fidgety, hunched over—and whittling away at a block of wood. Now, I unpacked his knife, some chunks of pinewood, and a carving that looked familiar.

In the narrow shaft of light from the doorway, I could see that it was a bird—lovely, round, and sleepy. One wing and one foot had not yet released themselves from the wood out of which the rest of the creature had emerged. Still, you could clearly sense the temper of this bird—utterly secure in itself, and at peace. It was not a gull—angular and shrill—but another kind of bird entirely. A bird from memory, from home.

How could a little ferret like Ottar . . . create *this*?

Or maybe a better question: How could someone who had *this* within him . . . choose to bind himself to the likes of Hauk?

On the other hand, I knew what it was to be afraid, to sacrifice honor for protection.

I sat back on my heels, now, fighting off the leaden weight of dread. I *might* be able to find my way to my father's people without the letter. But would they believe I was who I claimed to be, or would they take me for a fraud?

So, I would watch both of them—Hauk and Ottar—whenever I could, in hopes that they hadn't destroyed the letter but had secreted it somewhere else.

"Arthur! What are you doing here?"

The doctor! "I, uh . . ."

I was about to tell him about the letter, when Thorvald appeared in the doorway behind him. "There you are, Arthur! Sailing or bailing. Back to your post!"

Quickly, I tucked the little bird into Ottar's seabag and hied myself back to the hold.

\||//

Early that afternoon the wind picked up. The ship pitched hard; water formed sloshing waves in the hold. In a while, Thorvald came to bid me calm the bear, who had become restive. "Doctor says, 'Stay with her, and don't leave her.'"

As I emerged from below, I saw the storm—a mass of blue-gray clouds that blotted out the western horizon and boiled up to the roof of the sky. The captain stood on the sterncastle, bellowing out orders. Seamen swarmed all across the deck and up into the ratlines.

A cold rain began to fall.

The bear was pacing. I felt the running energy on her, a twitchy buzz that crackled in the air and echoed in my bones. I hummed to her for a while, but the humming held its own restless tremor, a tremor that comforted neither her nor me. A dark line blurred the horizon to the south—land. The Low Countries. If it came to the worst, if the ship sank . . .

Some of us could fit into the shore boat.

But not all.

I could swim, and likely there would be wreckage to cling to, and land couldn't be too far away.

But the bear, confined in her iron cage . . .

The doctor had ordered me to stay with her. But I had to speak with him—now.

I made my way across the deck, which was devilish slick and treacherous. Wind tore at my cloak, and rain like pea gravel pelted at my face. I had thought that the doctor might be attending to Ketil, and I wasn't wrong. As I entered the storeroom, the ship pitched, a lantern swung overhead, and light flooded the two men's faces. Ketil was breathing heavily, and blood oozed through the dressing cloths the doctor was applying. In a pail, I saw the old cloths, rust-red and sodden.

Would he live? I wondered. How could he, with so much blood lost . . .

I recalled how the bear had tossed the pirate into the air, like a child playing with a toy. The doctor was right. The bear was wild, dangerous, unpredictable. What had I been thinking, sleeping in her cage?

The doctor looked up. "Arthur, I sent word for you to see to the bear. You'd best get back there now."

"But—"

Ketil moaned in pain. It felt oddly wrong now to defend the bear in the presence of the man she had nearly slain. But someone had to defend her. And she was the king's bear, after all. It was the doctor's duty to save her.

"But the bear. What's your plan for—"

The doctor rolled Ketil onto his side; he let out

a cry. The doctor murmured to him, adjusted his dressings.

"—your plan for if we sink?"

Ketil started up from the deck, a feverish look in his eye. "Sink? Are we sinking?"

"No," the doctor said. "Don't fret; this is a good, sound ship, and we're well afloat." He pressed his hands against Ketil's shoulders; Ketil lay back down. The doctor set to work quickly tying the ends of the dressings to hold them in place. "Get along," he bade me. "You have work to do."

"But the bear will drown if—"

"Let it, then," Ketil said. "Let it drown! If I could get up off this pallet, I'd drown it with my own bare hands!"

"Off with you, Arthur!" the doctor said. "If worse comes to worst, we'll set the bear free and capture her later. But it's too soon for that. For now, we wait and see."

As I opened the door, a wind gust tore at my cloak and hurled a hard spray into my eyes. I squinted out toward the dim line of land to the south and then turned to face the storm looming to the west. It had grown nearer—darkening, eating up the sky.

We'd better not wait too long.

⇥ CHAPTER 25 ⇤

Storm

SOON THE STORM was full upon us.

The clamor of it filled my ears: the whistling of wind, the roar and hiss of waves, the pounding of rain. The ship pitched alarmingly, and the timbers ground and shuddered, as if they were trying to wrench themselves apart. The captain called to strike the sail. The land before us, which had been dimmed by the curtain of rain, now vanished entirely, blotted out by hill after looming hill of water.

I stayed beside the cage, not only because the doctor had ordered me to, but also because the cage was lashed securely to the deck, and the bars gave me something to hang on to. The bear came to huddle in the corner near where I stood; she grumbled deep in her throat in a way that sounded like complaining, as if telling me she wasn't pleased with things as now they stood. I told her I agreed with her and began to hum, not only to soothe her, but to comfort myself, as well.

Just after sunset, the seas gathered themselves into a single, towering wave that streamed white mist like the manes of galloping horses. The ship labored up the steep wall of water; the bear slid sternward in her cage, scrabbling at the cage floor, moaning piteously. I clung tight to the bars. A bailing bucket clattered past. A pot. A spoon. A boot.

And then suddenly, it was over; we had crested the wave. But hardly had I caught my breath before we were sliding into a deep trough, and another monstrous wave bore down upon us.

We were going to sink. I knew it now, with a certainty deep in the pit of my belly. If the pirate ship hadn't rammed us, we might have survived this storm, but we were listing, listing to starboard, and what had been a slight tilt before—a tilt with some buoyancy to it—was now a deep, leaden sluggishness, dragging us toward the bottom of the sea.

I heard shouting but could see only moving

shadows through the veil of rain and flying foam and spray. Were they heading for the shore boat? I stepped away from the cage for a better look, but then the deck shifted beneath my feet, tilted up the steep wall of the wave. My feet skated out from under me, and I was sliding—sliding like a turtle on my back, sliding astern. . . .

I slammed hard against the door of the captain's quarters. Water poured down the deck toward me. I tried to pull myself to my feet, but the ship bucked with a mighty thump, and I fell, cracking my head against the timbers. There were terrible creaking and groaning and splintering sounds, as if the world itself were being rent asunder; a wall of water crashed down upon me; the deck canted disastrously to starboard . . . and then it jerked hard and went still beneath me.

I wiped my eyes and blinked to clear them. Beneath the din of the ship, I could make out the boom and suck of beach waves, but they seemed distant, and I wondered if we had hit some offshore shoal or sandbar. I could see little in the dark and the rain, except that a black sheet of water was creeping across the starboard deck. Not waves, but the body of the sea itself.

I staggered to my feet and groped my way along the wall of the captain's quarters, toward the storeroom.

The helmsman, I saw, had fled, leaving the tiller unmanned. But the doctor would know what to do. At last, I reached the door, but it was jammed. I threw my weight against it; it yielded. "Doctor!" I said.

But he wasn't there. By the faint light of the lantern that swung from the rafters, I saw that Ketil was gone too, and in his place lay a tangle of dressings.

Had the doctor taken him to the shore boat?

A breaker crashed over the stern. The ship shuddered; shadows leaped and swayed across the cabin; I clutched the doorjamb to keep my balance. And then, amidst the rush and boom of seawater, I heard the bear: a great, long, sorrowful bellow that rose in an accusation of betrayal.

And who could blame her?

There might still be hope for me, but the bear . . .

The bear, who knew how to swim, who was *born* to swim in cold, open waters . . .

The bear would be dragged down under the sea to drown.

CHAPTER 26

Keys

WHERE WERE THE keys?

I had seen them in the doctor's wooden chest when he was stitching up the bear. But where . . . ?

I scanned the room. The seabags, bedrolls, and sea chests had scattered all across the deck. I'd never find that chest! And the doctor might have taken it. . . .

A wave boomed against the stern; a sudden flare of light . . .

There. On the wall. A ring of keys hanging from a nail.

Another wave. Water poured into the storeroom; the ship shifted, tilted. Steeply to starboard, and astern.

Go!

I snatched up the keys and fled.

\\\//

Outside, the moon slipped from behind the massed clouds, revealing gusting drifts of rain. I could hear shouts and thumps and creaking; I could hear water gurgling below. My feet skidded on the wet boards. Another wave hit astern. I slipped, fell, careened down, down, down into the cold water on the starboard deck and then fetched up against something hard—a bollard. I crawled back up toward the bear.

She turned to look at me. Let out a small, indignant grunt.

I found the padlock among the chains that held the door.

Another wave. I clung to a cage bar and fumbled with the keys. I stabbed one at the slot in the padlock. It wouldn't go. Tried a second. A third.

Another wave.

Hold tight to the bar. Stay on your feet.

Two more keys I tried, and at last, a fit.

The grinding of the tumblers.

Click!

My fingers plucked at the chains; I unwound them loop by loop. The door swung open.

Another wave. The ship shuddered and screeched. And the bear was sliding toward me—scraping her claws against the cage floor. She hurtled across the threshold, knocking into the door. It swung, slammed against my elbow, sent pain jolting up and down my arm. My hand loosed the bar, and I was slipping down across the canted deck toward the water that had come to live there, slipping into it, up to my neck. My feet felt the deck at a steep slant far beneath me; my knees felt the hard curve of the starboard rail, but then it dropped away entirely, and there was nothing, nothing but water all around.

≋ CHAPTER 27 ≋

Some Kind of Dream

WATER SLAPPED AT me, blinding me, filling my mouth and nose. I thrashed my arms and legs and rose to the surface, choking, gasping for air. Rain thundered on the surface of the sea. The waves foamed and hissed. I looked about me but could see nothing but water.

Shouting. I thought I heard my name. And then another wave hit me, I went under again. I kicked hard, broke to the surface.

"Help!" I called.

My voice sounded small in my ears. I kicked again, rode to the top of a wave. There. Behind me, a dark shape against the sky—the ship. I shouted again, louder, but sank into a trough between waves. The dark shape vanished.

Voices. Fainter now.

A cold tide of panic flooded me. Blindly, I struck out toward where I had last seen the ship. I called again . . . and a large, pale mass glided through the water beneath me.

A seal?

A squid?

A whale?

No.

It was the bear.

She rose to the surface just beside me. I reached out and grabbed the strip of harness on her back.

Would she shake me off? Turn round to bite me? Dive deep into the sea to dislodge me?

I didn't know.

She stroked powerfully through the water, and I could feel the pulse of the running thrum in her, the restless force that had been pent up for so long. I could feel that she was doing exactly what she wanted and needed to do—to run, run, run through the water until the humming eased out of her blood.

At first I held on only with my hands; I didn't want to straddle her, because she might find that disrespectful—and besides, no one rides a bear. But the sea pulled and tugged and slapped at me, trying to shove me away. So, I pressed my body into hers—arms about her neck, fingers clutching fur and harness, legs splayed, feet clinging to her sides.

I watched for waves and breathed in just before they broke over us, for the bear often tunneled deep beneath them. I held my breath when it seemed my lungs would burst. The world shrank down to a single slope of water rising before me, to the feel of fur and leather in my hands, to the taste of salt in my mouth, to the smell of wet bear, to the cold hard pelting of rain like pebbles on my back.

Soon my fingers went numb, but I willed them to stay clenched. Dimly, I became aware of a new sound—a low rumbling that seemed at first like the pulse of blood in my veins, but worked its way through the dullness of my mind until it became a roaring sound that I knew well:

Surf.

I raised my head and saw a slantwise, chalk-white line of foam before me, and beyond that, a deeper blackness in a smooth, wide swath.

Land.

And it seemed that I must have been living in some

kind of dream, a dream where I was riding a great pale bear through the sea, a bear who was taking me to shore. Yes, it had to be a dream, but I was too weary to wake from it, so I held my breath through the tumult of the pounding waves, and when I found the sand beneath my feet, I slipped off the bear and stumbled up the beach—with my numb toes, with my numb feet, with my numb knees. I lay down in a patch of seagrass, and then, for a while, I knew no more.

PART III

THE LOW
COUNTRIES

CHAPTER 28

Alone

THERE WAS THE sound of the sea—the dull, hollow roar of it—and the drag of sand and pebbles on the shore. There was the moon, dim and far. There was the rich, deep smell of something wild and feral, and the brush of fur against my arm. There was the thirst that never ended; and the waves of chills that coursed through my body; and the hot, hot burning of my skin.

I moved in and out of dreams. It seemed in one moment that my mother was there, crying, "Arthur! Where are you?"; and in the next that I was stumbling up a rocky shore toward the sound of running water. My stepbrothers came and taunted me for my clumsiness, and a great white bear lumbered up to me and said, "Eat." Then I was in the sea, calling to the shrinking ship until it disappeared beneath the waves. Once, the doctor came to me and shouted instructions I couldn't comprehend. Another time I saw a dark-eyed man with a deeply familiar face watching over me with a grave and kindly smile.

.I came blearily awake to a sharp pain in my hip. I rolled off the thing that had been digging into me—a stone. I blinked and looked about. The waning moon hung above, behind the dark, thin fingers of stunted trees. I could hear a stream nearby, and the distant throb of the surf.

I felt pitifully weak and empty.

Against my back pressed something solid but not hard. I could feel it breathing, rocking me like a boat on a rolling sea. I smelled its familiar smell. . . .

The bear.

Was I dreaming still?

I closed my eyes, and a great peace moved through my body, lapping over me in cool blue waves, gentle as a rising tide.

\\\\/

When next I woke, I was shivering. I breathed in, and did not smell *bear*—only the salt tang of the sea, and the sweet green perfume of new growth. I listened, and did not hear breathing—only the hum of insects, and a gurgling of water, and the distant rumble of breaking waves. I leaned back and did not feel the bear's solid bulk—only a cold emptiness where she had been.

I opened my eyes. Clambered stiffly to my feet. My hair felt frigid and wet; I wiped droplets of moisture off my face.

It was daytime, but a close, dense mist hovered just above the ground, draining light and color from the world. I could see that I stood on a small, rocky knoll, surrounded by a few twisted, dead trees and a screen of scrubby alder brush and tall marsh grasses. That gurgle of water must mean that a stream ran nearby, but I couldn't see it through the mist.

I tried to patch together a memory of how I had come to this place.

The shipwreck.

The keys.

The bear.

How long had I been here? One day? Two? A week?

My head felt strange, a little dizzy. The fever and chills seemed to have passed, but I felt stupid and slow, and all my strength had seeped out of me. My cloak and tunic and shirt felt damp. I had no boots, and my cap and knife had vanished.

I followed the murmur of water to the stream; I knelt and drank.

When I sat up, my head had cleared a little.

A feather of breeze brushed my face; the mist swirled, parting briefly to show a broad expanse of sand beyond the thicket; the tide must be out. And then the shroud drew close about me again.

I was alone. Completely.

I called out—some pitiful sound, not even a word. I rose to my feet and called again. For the doctor. For the captain. For the bear. I stumbled through the trees and down to the beach, fog clotting thick about me. I scanned up and down the shore, but all I could see was blank sand upon which no footsteps were writ in either direction.

"Halloo!" I cried. "Is anyone here? Help!"

A seabird, invisible in the sky above me, let out a hoarse and lonely cry.

All at once, the running hum quickened within me—drumming in my blood, jangling in my bones. I took off at a trot along the shore, my feet clumsy and leaden in the sand. I searched again for footprints, for the looming shape of the wrecked *Queen Margrete*, for marks where the shore boat might have been dragged across the sand, for lean-tos, fire pits, bear prints or scat—for any sign that I wasn't the only living soul left on God's Earth. I ran until my knees buckled, until my breath came ragged and short, until a sharp pain stabbed at my side.

I collapsed onto the beach, panting. My limbs shook, and my head felt light. When at last I caught my breath, I twisted round and looked back from whence I had come.

A trail of footprints etched a solitary line in the sand and disappeared into the fog.

Mine.

The thunder and boom of the waves rumbled in my ears. It was the same body of water I had known for most of my life—the North Sea—but the land itself was foreign. I rose to my feet, brushing wet sand off my hands.

Something shuddered, deep within me.

For so long, I had merely played at running away, but now, at last I had truly done so. I was alone, entirely. With no one to mock me or command me. With no one to pummel me with fist and foot, or keep me from the work I coveted. With no one to care for me or protect me.

Even the bear had deserted me.

I took a deep breath.

Think. Think what to do.

I must have fetched up in the Low Countries, south of the North Sea. If the shore boat had reached land, it might not be far from here. Maybe the men were still nearby. Maybe the doctor would be looking for me.

If he had survived . . .

I brushed the thought away.

I didn't feel hungry, but I knew I needed food. In any case, there was fresh water in the stream, and my throat felt parched.

And the bear . . .

Had the bear truly taken me to shore, or had I dreamed it? I remembered the warm feel of her pressed against my back on the knoll, and the oddly comforting sound of her breathing.

A sudden pang struck my heart at the thought that the bear had abandoned me.

Don't be a fool, I told myself. She was a bear and had gone off to save herself.

What else would you expect a bear to do?

CHAPTER 29

Brown-Haired Lass

THE FOG HAD begun to dissipate when I returned to the place where the stream met the sea. I recognized the shape of the knoll, and the scrubby alder thicket. But now I saw what I had missed before: a line of tracks leading down from the knoll and into the wide, wet sands.

Bear tracks.

They vanished into the fog farther out, where water had seeped up and filled them. But . . .

Maybe she hadn't left me. Maybe she had just gone looking for food.

I squinted out toward the sea, but the fog, though

thinner now, still blurred the world beyond the tracks, and I could find neither shipwreck nor bear.

Well, the bear might find prey in the sea, but if I were to scavenge myself a meal, it would have to be on land.

\\\\//

It was the birds that showed me where to find it. I followed the sound of their calls, tramping inland across a flat marshy plain of meadow flowers and grasses. The fog dwindled to a scrim of feathery patches and then vanished altogether. The land grew drier beneath my feet, and before long, I found the birds converged upon a high, broad hummock of brambles flecked with deep purple berries. I clapped my hands to startle them away, for they were thick upon the berries, but these birds did not scare easily. I ran at them, flailing about with my arms; the ones closest to me chattered indignantly, then hopped a little way off and kept on feeding. I picked a berry and tasted it. Some kind of blackberry, probably, though we never saw them in Norway this early in June. It was perfectly ripe—yielding to the tooth but not mushy. The sweet juice puddled on my tongue. At the taste of it, hunger wakened like a beast within me. The word *poison* fluttered into my mind, but I told myself that birds wouldn't eat poisonous berries. I plowed through the bushes and, ignoring scratching thorns and scattering birds, picked one handful of berries after another and stuffed them into my mouth.

The sun beat down, warming me. My belly began to feel full. After a while, I heard voices, faint and far away. High, fluting voices. Children's voices.

I looked about me and saw a twist of woodsmoke in the distance, to the west. No, there were two, three, four of them, clustered all together.

A village?

My heart lifted. I had a sudden vision of friendly villagers welcoming me to their hearths, urging me to sit at their table.

But . . . they might *not* be friendly. What manner of people lived here, I did not know. They might be heathens, or . . .

Just then, I heard a sudden rustling in the bushes, surprisingly near. And a girl's voice, in some foreign tongue. I froze, torn between fleeing and standing my ground, and then she appeared out of the tangle of berries—a brown-haired lass in a moss-green gown—and a much younger boy toddling sturdily behind. The girl made a startled sound and stared at me. Then the boy pointed at me and began to babble, his words rising in pitch, like a question. The girl seemed to rouse herself from her startlement. She spoke to me as well, but her words cut sharp—a challenge. She thrust an arm in my direction, and I saw she was holding a long, curved knife, the kind used for cutting forage.

I smiled and held up my hands, to show I meant no ill. I pointed toward the sea and made a gesture that I hoped conveyed the notion of a ship. The girl watched me intently. I guessed they might know Latin, but my own Latin was thin. I said the Latin word for *sea*. I said the Latin word for *boat*.

A look of understanding spread across the girl's face. She nodded, pointing with the knife back toward the sea, only in a more easterly direction from where I had fetched up. She repeated the word for boat emphatically.

Might she have seen the shore boat?

The girl was repeating *boat* again, when she seemed to catch sight of something over my shoulder. Her eyes widened; the knife dropped from her hand. She turned and, yanking on the little imp's arm, made for a gap in the berry bushes and disappeared.

I whipped round to see what had alarmed her and saw a great white shape loping across the field toward us.

The bear.

⪢ CHAPTER 30 ⪡

Galumphing Grace

SHE RAN WITH an easy, galumphing grace, and I halfway wanted to follow the children into the berry bushes, and I halfway wanted to go to the bear and greet her, because she was the closest thing I had to a friend in this place. She had left me unharmed in her cage. She had borne me through the sea. She had slept beside me and warmed me. Still, a clamoring of inner voices said, *She's a bear! Run! Run!*

But my stepfather had told me never to run from a bear, because you will look like prey. And an ice bear can outrun you every time. So I forced myself to be still, to root my feet to the ground.

She slowed as she approached me. She made a little grunting sound, a sound like a welcome. She stretched out her head toward me and shook it in a way that seemed almost playful. She grunted again and then brushed past me, filling my nose with the scent of her. She began sniffing along the edge of the brambles.

All the air whooshed out of me. I hadn't truly thought she would harm me, but still . . .

Something glinted down low in the mass of bushes where the girl and the boy had disappeared. On the ground: the girl's curved knife. I picked it up, ran a finger along the blade. It was a good knife, sharp and clean. And my knife probably lay on the bottom of the sea.

The bear was rummaging deep into the bramble patch, holding the branches with her paws and sweeping up ripe berries with her tongue.

All at once, her head whipped up. She sniffed at the air, seeming puzzled.

Voices. Deeper ones this time.

Four or five men and boys appeared at a distance, beyond the brambles. Some of them began to shout and wave their arms like henwives driving their birds.

The bear turned to me, as if to ask what I made of this strange behavior.

A stocky man with a bushy, russet-colored beard

reached for something behind his back—and nocked an arrow in his bow.

The bear wheeled round and crashed through the bushes, toward me. An arrow arced high in the air and, with a sickening *thunk*, embedded itself into her flank.

She roared. The man loosed three more arrows in quick succession; one zinged by me so close, I felt it sting my ear.

The bear hurtled past, and still clutching the girl's knife, I took off running too.

CHAPTER 31

Running

FOR A WHILE I could see the bear before me, running, with a lazy, rolling gait that nonetheless left me far behind. And then it was only her tracks that I could see—the flattened trail in the reeds and grasses, heading east. At first I thought I heard voices calling behind me, but before long, I heard only the swish and crunch of the grass beneath my feet, the cries of seabirds, the sound of my own breath coming fast.

I looked back and saw no one following, but I didn't stop. It felt good to be running—running hard and far. Running from the arrows, from the men and the boys. Running from Hauk, from the captain. Running from my stepbrothers, my stepfather. Just running—moving across the meadow, smelling dirt and crushed reeds, watching clouds drift overhead in a still, blue summer sky.

In time, the ground went marshy underfoot. I slowed down, picking my way from hummock to stone to stump, trying not to sink into the mire. The soles of my feet, which had held up well in the grass, began to smart. A cloud of swarming insects buzzed about my head. My throat felt parched, but this water was thick with mud, impossible to drink.

I dragged to a halt. The running thrum had burned itself out. The bear had disappeared long before, as had her tracks, and now I stood ringed about with sedge and rushes. My legs felt shaky, and my stomach, hollow. A bird chirped, and a small wind rattled in the reeds. I was alone, completely.

What to do now?

Before the bear had appeared, the brown-haired lass had seemed friendly. If not for the bear, would her people have taken me in? Fed me? Given me house-room for a while? Maybe if I went back there . . .

I touched a finger to my wounded ear. It came away wet. The cut didn't seem serious—just a nick—but still. A hand's length to the left, and I would have been dead.

They might not have intended me harm, but they

were willing to kill me if I got in the way.

If only the fog hadn't been so dense! The ship had run aground on something; maybe it hadn't sunk entirely. Maybe the crew were there right now, salvaging what they might. And surely they'd come looking for me.

Or at least, they'd come looking for the bear.

The doctor . . .

If he'd survived . . .

I slapped at a stinging fly. The sky to the east was going dim, though the sun glowed softly gold in the west, whence I had come. There was no sign of people, nor even the smoke I had seen earlier. And my tracks had disappeared in the marsh.

A bubble of fear began to swell within me. What should I do?

To the east, beyond the swish of grasses, I could hear a purl of water. More faintly, to the north, the dim roar and hiss of the sea.

First, find fresh water to drink. Then decide: to look for the village . . . or make my way back to the coast and search for the ship and crew.

\\\\//

In a while the breeze parted the reeds, revealing a wide stream. I slaked my thirst, and afterward sat back on my heels. I was hungry. It had been hours since I'd had those berries, and they hadn't been nearly enough.

A splash. I looked upstream, and there she was, the bear—the whole huge white mass of her. She stood on a rock in the water, looking so unlikely and out of place here that again I felt as if I had stepped out of the common, ordinary world and into a dream.

She regarded me, seeming unsurprised, and then gave me a soft, snuffling grunt of greeting.

Had she come looking for me? Had she known where I was all along?

I was surprised at how good it felt to see her, to find myself not entirely alone.

She turned back to the stream. The arrow, I saw, still bristled from her flank, but it didn't seem to trouble her. In a moment she lunged headfirst into the water. She emerged, shaking herself off, and I half expected to see a fish between her jaws, but there was nothing.

I recalled something the hunters had said when they visited the steading—that ice bears are skilled at catching seals but not fish.

She must be hungry too.

So, then, was I safe with her? She had never offered me harm, but still . . . She had been well-fed on the boat but not now. And I knew from the hunters' tales that there's no animal on Earth more perilous than a hungry ice bear.

But this one had saved my life.

That girl, the brown-haired lass . . . she had said *boat* in Latin. If the doctor and sailors had come seeking us, the shore boat might still be beached on the sand. Or maybe she had seen the *Queen Margrete*?

So, I would go back to the sea, and search.

It was all I could think to do.

CHAPTER 32

Piggy Eyes

I FOLLOWED THE stream north, toward the sea, halfway hoping the bear would go her own way. But each time I stopped, she appeared behind me. At last, as dusk thickened, I settled down in a patch of tall grass, out of sight, some distance from her.

If she were going to harm me, she would have done it well before now.

Wouldn't she?

I looked about and saw a thin column of smoke, still to the west, but closer to where I was now than the last smoke I had seen. What could it be? Another village, or . . . ?

Nearby, I heard the bear trampling a place in the grass and grunting as she lay down. Soon, I heard another sound, a curious *rumph, rumph, rumph.*

What was she doing?

I stood, and cautiously made my way through the reeds toward her.

Sprawled out on the ground near the streambank, she had twisted her head back and was worrying at the base of the arrow shaft like a dog digging out fleas.

I tiptoed away from her and lay down in my sleeping place.

Rumph, rumph, rumph.

The doctor had said the pirates' arrows would fester if they weren't removed. But there was nothing I could do about it. Maybe . . . maybe she would pull out the arrow herself.

After a time the sound ended. I lay awake listening— to the chirrup of frogs and the call of some alien bird, to the rustle of small creatures in the bushes. A chill seeped up from the damp ground; shivering, I drew my cloak tightly about me. Away in the distance a wolf howled.

My feet throbbed with pain from cuts and bruises, and I longed for my boots. Worse, the berries did not sit well with me; my belly was grinding and growling.

If I were home, I thought, Mama would make me a potion of chamomile. She would sit beside me until I went to sleep.

Mama . . .

I had had to leave her. Didn't I?

I closed my eyes, and *his* face floated up before me, the dark-eyed man who had appeared to me when I was ill.

Father.

I imagined riding through a deep forest with him, with Prince David. The smells of leather and pine and damp moss. My father's voice.

Son.

But the voice I heard in my mind . . . was the doctor's.

What had become of him? Had he survived the wreck?

I should take to my heels, now, before the bear awakened, to find the doctor or others from the ship and tell them where to find the bear. They would be grateful that I had saved her, wouldn't they? The *king* would be grateful. Maybe they would give me a reward. . . .

And then, Wales . . . The letter was gone, but people would remember my father. Surely someone could tell me where to find my kin and the land that was my birthright. Surely I could persuade them I was my father's son.

I rose to my feet. I heard the stream gurgling past, and the musical *ploink* as a frog jumped into the water. I heard the buzz of some nighttime insect. The moon had hidden behind a patch of dark clouds; I couldn't tell which way was west.

A snorting sound.

The crunch of trampled undergrowth.

The moon slid out from behind the clouds, and then I saw it: a pair of dark eyes gleaming in the grasses, not an arm's length away.

The hump of a large, bristly back.

The bright sweep of a pair of tusks.

More snorting. More tusks. More small, piggy eyes.

Wild boars. Five of them, at least. Staring straight at me.

A small, frightened sound escaped my lips, and I went cold, all down the back of me. I knew it would be foolish to run, for the boars would come after me, and those tusks could tear a full-grown man to bits.

I breathed in their pungent smell and sensed the heat coming off the dense, knuckled mass of their bodies. Slowly, I reached for the knife, though little good it would do me.

The biggest boar snorted, moved closer.

And then, just behind me, a growl—rumbling, fathoms deep. I turned round to see the bear.

A crashing in the underbrush; the eyes vanished in a whisper of moving grasses.

The bear grunted, as if to say, *There. And good riddance to them.* She glanced in the direction the boars had gone, and then snuffled all up and down the front of me. She grunted again and then lay down in the grass at my feet, the arrow still sticking out from her flank.

I drew in a deep breath, then another. My bloodbeat began to calm. A breeze rattled in the reeds; I shivered. I lay down, near enough to smell the bear, near enough to feel the welcome warmth that surrounded her body. She didn't make a sound, didn't turn to look at me. But one of her hind feet reached out behind her and pressed its furry pads flat against my side. I felt myself relax against her feet, and a wave of comfort went rolling through me. I began to hum to her, as I had done before.

This place was safe for me only because of the bear. There were wolves out there, as well as boars. And maybe other wild animals too.

There would be no going back toward the shore alone tonight. For now, I needed the bear more than she needed me.

≢ CHAPTER 33 ≝

A Great, Wide Bay

I WOKE TO a splashing sound and jumped to my feet to see the bear in midstream, shaking off water. And between her jaws . . . a fish! She set it down on the rocks and, holding it down with one paw, ripped off pieces and devoured them. Then she clambered onto a boulder and peered into the stream. In a moment she flopped in headfirst, sending cascades of water in all directions and, after much thrashing about, reappeared with another fish.

She looked so clumsy, I almost wanted to laugh. On the other hand I'd never heard tell of an ice bear catching fish in a stream.

The next few tries, she missed. But then she caught one again, dropped it on the streambank. She turned to look at me, grunted, and lumbered in again.

The fish was flopping about, alive. But . . . had she caught it for me?

I hesitated. If I tried to take it, and *she* wanted it . . .

But she climbed back onto the rock again, and soon had another fish.

So the one on the bank . . . was for me.

I snatched it before she could change her mind, and ran off a little way to a small, reedy knoll, where I slammed the fish against a rock and killed it. The girl's curved knife was a clumsy tool for my purpose, but I managed to pare away scales and bones, and hack off fins and head. The fish was large, and what remained, though cold and greasy and unpleasant on my tongue, filled the empty hollow in my belly.

When I finished I lay back in the grass, feeling stronger than I had since the shipwreck. A light breeze ruffled the reeds, and a rill of liquid birdsong caught my ear. The smoke from the night before had vanished. Likely not another village, then. Likely a traveler, one who had moved on. I breathed in the sweet air, full of the smell of clean water and mud and grasses in new, spring leaf. Those boars hadn't sought me out; they had only met with me by chance in their nighttime foraging. If I kept my wits about me, I could stay out of their way. And the bear . . . She was no longer hungry, and she seemed to see me as her own.

So I would go north, to the coast, and then back west along the shore, searching for the *Queen Margrete* or the shore boat or some other sign of the crew. If the bear continued to follow me, I would stay clear of the village. But I was bound to find some trace of my crewmates, wasn't I? And then . . . I would help them recapture the bear for the king.

\\\\\/

I trudged along beside the stream until it got lost in a reed-clogged pond, then I made my own path in a northerly direction through the sedges. The soles of my feet felt swollen and raw, but they didn't pain me so much as the day before, and walking drove the chill from my bones. I flushed a duck from her nest and dined on a few of her eggs; I foraged for berries. This country was studded with swampy patches, ponds, and streams—neither entirely land nor wholly marsh—and often enough I found myself bogged to the knees.

At first I thought the bear might have gone her own way. But in a little while she appeared off to one side of me, shuffling through the willow brush, dining on eggs and berries, like me. She was no longer white, but covered with mud. Her great head swung from side to side as she walked, and while the arrow still bristled from her flank, it didn't seem to trouble her. From time to time she halted to look about, raising her nose to the wind. Sometimes she broke out in a burst of speed for no reason, romping through the shallow water. Once, she rose up onto her hind legs and surveyed the land before us, looking for all the world like a human person—maybe the captain of a sailing ship scanning the horizon for the sight of land.

Before long I heard the rumble of waves in the distance, and soon smelled the salt of sea air. The thrum of the running energy took hold of me; I jogged across the field, to the shore. The tide had ebbed; sand stretched out smooth and gleaming for what seemed like leagues, reaching nearly to a chain of islands at the horizon.

Islands!

I'd thought the *Queen Margrete* had fetched up on a reef. But what if it had been an island?

I scanned the islands for signs of a wreck, but they stretched far in both directions, impossible to see clearly.

Out of the corner of my eye, I caught sight of something moving. The bear. She loped across the sand toward the sea. Beyond her, to the east—a patch of silver-bright water reaching far inland. A great, wide bay. Across the waters . . . Something . . . A town?

I set out at a trot toward the bay, hoping to see more clearly. Yes, a small town or fishing village. I could see the small dark humps of boats snuggled up in the harbor. And, in the middle of the bay . . . a single, larger vessel. Familiar. Longer and sleeker than a cog, with faded, red-on-gold stripes on the sail. And it was listing to starboard . . .

At once, I knew. I was looking at the *Queen Margrete*.

CHAPTER 34

Honorary Bear

I JUMPED STRAIGHT up and whooped. The *Queen Margrete!* What a glorious stroke of luck! I stared at the ship, making sure I had seen aright. The shape of the hull, the sail . . . If this wasn't the *Queen Margrete*, it was her double. And listing to starboard . . .

She must have gone aground—not sunk. And somehow, over these past few days, they must have repaired her well enough so that she could limp into port.

I scanned the bay, trying to gauge how long it would take to walk around it and come to the village. The land stretched out flat and reedy as far as the eye could see—except for a few scattered, tree-topped knolls. Who knew how much was bog or stream or pond that must be skirted? It would be a full day, at least. Maybe more.

They would likely take longer than that to repair her, but . . .

The *Queen Margrete!*

I had to reach her—and soon—before she set sail again.

\\\\//

I set off south, along the edge of the bay. I did not wait for the bear, because I knew she would find me if she wanted to. I tried not to think of nighttime visits by boars but only of the *Queen Margrete*.

The sun warmed me as I walked, and a fragrant breeze cooled my face. The marsh was alive with birds and frogs and dragonflies and clouds of stinging insects. I kept a sharp eye out for snakes.

Shadows lengthened. Still no bear.

A loon called, eerie and sad, reaching down to a cavern of loneliness deep at the center of me.

Had the bear left me? Did she decide to go off on her own?

But late that afternoon I heard a crashing in the reeds—and there she was—her flanks and underbelly mud-caked, and her muzzle and neck rusty with blood. So it wasn't just fish she had been eating. She gave a grunt of greeting and came romping toward me, huge and wild and fast. A geyser of panic spurted up within me—but I nailed my feet to the ground and told myself to trust her.

Sure enough, she skidded to a halt before me. She snuffled at my chest, my face, my hair, smearing me with mud and blood. She pushed the top of her head against me, like old Loki when he wanted me to scratch his ears.

I hesitated, then lightly stroked her, then dug my fingers deep into her fur, scraping my nails against her black skin. She turned her head so that I was scratching behind her wounded ear. She let out a contented little snort. I breathed in deep.

Truth to tell, I was glad to see her, too.

\|||/

Evening came, and we still hadn't reached the southernmost end of the bay. The bear dug a small pit in the sand, lay down in it, and began to worry at the arrow. *Rumph, rumph, rumph.* I feared it might be festering, but told myself that soon, if all went well, the bear would be with the doctor, and he would pull it out.

I lay down some distance away from her but,

remembering the boars, crept nearer. My feet felt numb with cold, save for a sharp pain on my left sole. I prized out a thorn there and eased the sting with a poultice of wet sand.

After a while the bear stretched out on one side, and her great paws began to twitch. I watched until she settled down, until her back rose and fell in the slow rhythms of sleep breathing.

I closed my eyes and imagined walking into the village with the king's great ice bear following at my heels, and the whole crew cheering because I had saved our expedition from failure. Well, I knew it wouldn't come to pass just so. The bear might not follow me into a village. She might well be slain if she did. I'd have to slip away from her, somehow, and alert the doctor. But still . . . I pictured the doctor welcoming us back. Surely he'd be glad to see us.

Son.

I could see the captain bestowing a heap of silver coins upon me, and maybe a medal, too. Better still: I imagined Hauk slinking off into some dark corner with his tail between his legs.

The bear gave a snort. She rolled over onto her belly, closer to me, and pressed one warm, furry foot-pad against my leg. As if she wanted to make sure I was still there. As if she were watching out for me.

My imaginings collapsed, and a thrum of uncertainty wormed its way into my chest. A night bird called, sounding harsh and strange. Something splashed in a nearby pond, and a small breeze stirred the grasses.

I gazed at the bear, the bear of whom I ought to have been afraid. But this bear knew me, protected me, fed me—like some magical creature from the old stories. As if she considered me . . . well, not precisely a bear like herself, but an *honorary* bear.

Away in the distance, a wolf howled, then another, sending a cold shiver up my spine. But the bear didn't so much as flick an ear.

And why should she be afraid? And why should I, with her to protect me?

Something heavy sloughed off me, like a mountain shrugging off a mass of wet snow. I had survived pirates and a shipwreck. I had escaped a hail of arrows. I had run with a great ice bear. There was no one to mock me, to strike me, to tell me where I had to be or what I had to do. I had no master now; I was free.

And yet . . .

I harked back to the day when I led the bear back into her cage on the ship. How the bars had crowded in upon me. How the cage roof had darkened the sky.

A chorus of wolves howled together, and the feeling of disquiet stirred again, burrowing its way deep within.

≋ CHAPTER 35 ≋

Sound Like a Whip

THE NEXT MORNING, when I awoke, I marked it again: a thin column of smoke to the west, twisting into the sky. But it seemed even closer than before.

Was someone following us?

Tracking us?

The *Queen Margrete*, though, lay in the opposite direction—to the east and north. And if someone from the ship had been following all along, coming to rescue us, why wouldn't he show himself? Surely he would have caught up to us by now, if he had wanted to.

We had been seen by others—the brown-haired

lass and the men who had shot at the bear. But why would they follow us?

Unless they craved bear meat and a fine white pelt . . .

The bear lifted her nose, sniffed at the wind.

"Come on, Bear," I said, "let's be off." Maybe there was no cause for worry. But the sooner we reached the *Queen Margrete*, the better I would feel.

\|||/

When at last we neared the southern shore of the bay, the bear suddenly veered and took off loping toward a copse of birches on a knoll a little way ahead. The wind bent the tops of the reeds and grasses, made them whisper and dance. Thin white clouds scudded across the sky, and in the distance, darker ones massed, portents of coming rain. As the sun rose high overhead, gleaming like pewter on the surface of the water, the bear disappeared into the trees.

I heard a strange sound, then, as I drew near—a sound like a whip, and then a startled kind of grunt. Rustling, thumping noises. Suddenly, the bear cried out—a cry of rage, or maybe pain—with a pleading note at the end that twisted like a fishhook in my gut.

I ran.

Shadows fell over me, webbing the ground with

darkness. But she was easy to spot among the trees, the great pale bulk of her moving strangely—jerky and hunched. Above her, something dark hung down from a branch, suspended from a rope. It was . . . part of a dead animal.

Bait.

I knew what to look for now; my eyes found the rope that led from a birch tree to the bear's hind leg.

A snare.

The bear heaved and buckled and thrashed, fighting against the rope. The tree shivered, showering down leaves.

She saw me coming, lunged toward me. Calling out, as you would call to a friend for help. The rope pulled her up short. She slashed at it, bit at it. Her leg, I saw, was bleeding. She lunged again, twisting it at an unnatural angle.

She was going to hurt herself if I didn't cut her loose.

Again, she lunged, and I circled round to the far side of the tree. There was nothing to prevent her from crushing me, but if I could keep the tree between us . . . I reached for the knife in my belt, slipped the tip of it under the rope that girded the trunk, and began to saw through.

The rope was thick and strong. The bear crashed against the tree, making it tremble, and quaking the earth beneath my feet. I jumped back, out of the way. She recoiled and rammed her shoulder into the tree trunk, then staggered back, seeming dazed. Quickly, I slipped my blade under the rope and began to saw at it again. One by one, the strands began to sever. When only a few threads remained, the bear lunged hard away and, with a snap, she was free.

She bolted through the copse, a length of rope dragging behind her. My heartbeat clattered in my chest; my legs and arms had gone to jelly. I peered up into the tree branches and made out a sleek, black animal head, and part of a shoulder. . . .

A seal.

Bait for an ice bear.

The trapper wouldn't be far—maybe just enough to keep from alarming the bear with his scent. But he would be back, and soon.

Through a cage of tree trunks, I could see the bear growing smaller in the distance, the arrow still sticking out from her flank. And all at once my heart brimmed over with some raw, tender sensation I could not name.

She had been stolen from her home for one king

to give to another. She had been slashed with knives, shot with arrows, trapped in this snare.

In my mind's eye, I saw her carefree, pigeon-toed shuffle across the marsh. I saw her rearing up on hind legs to her full height, looking about and drinking in the smells on the wind. I saw her scattering the wild boars and felt her furry foot pressed gently against my back at night.

And now the running energy was filling me up, was thrumming in my feet, my legs, my heart.

I ran.

⇛ CHAPTER 36 ⇚

Lopsided Hitch

WHEN I CAME out of the trees, I saw the bear bolting toward the water, a narrow inlet off the southernmost tip of the bay, into which a wide river flowed. The dark clouds had spread across the sky, blotting out the sun.

There was something different about her gait, a kind of lopsided hitch. It wasn't just the trapline trailing from her leg and snagging in logs and bushes. It wasn't just that she stopped from time to time to nip at the rope. It wasn't that she staggered a little, seeming confused. No, I could see that she was injured; she limped.

I ran after, and caught up to her at last near the

banks of the bay as she stopped again to worry at the noose around her leg. She turned to look at me and grunted a grunt that told me that she trusted me, that she thought I might be able to help. I squatted beside her, began to hum. Blood caked the matted fur on her leg. I plucked at the noose, but it was embedded deep, past fur and into skin. I feared that if I pulled too hard, it might make her bleed even more.

The tail of the rope had collected clumps of reeds and moss and fallen branches, which the bear had dragged behind her like an anchor. At least I could cut that short. I took the knife from my belt and sliced it through. The bear sniffed at my hands, then nuzzled my neck and my hair.

A shout. I jumped up to see a man running toward us from the west. I caught the gleam of knives at his belt; I saw a web of ropes dangling from one shoulder; I took in his bushy, russet beard. . . .

Familiar . . .

The man with the bow and arrows? The one who had shot the bear?

Now she heaved herself to her feet and made for the bay at a stumbling run. The man called out something I didn't understand, and then called again:

"Arthur!"

But how did he know . . . ?

Behind me, a splash. The man called my name again; I slipped the knife in my belt, turned my back on him, and flung myself into the bay. I kicked hard, reaching for the bear's harness, and clung to it as she stroked through the water and toward the far shore.

≡ CHAPTER 37 ≡

Stealing from the King

BY THE TIME we reached land, a light rain had begun to fall. The bear stumbled up onto the verge and, with a groan, sprawled out on her belly. I let go of her harness and collapsed against her side. I could feel her breathing against me, and the aura of heat that surrounded her. I could hear rain pattering on the ground beside me, and the splash of small waves against the shore. I could smell bear and mud and the lush green of fresh new grass.

I knew I should get up, but I didn't want to.

I knew I should lead the bear toward the village where the ship was docked, but I didn't want to.

I knew I should turn her in to the captain, but I didn't want to.

The bear moaned and shifted; I sat up. She began to lick at her leg near the trapline noose. A ragged mat of seagrasses had wound itself around the rope; beneath, I could see blood clotted and seeping in bubbles on the black of her skin.

A slow tide of anger began to rise within my chest.

Who had done this to her?

That man with the russet beard—the trapper—had known my name. So, had someone from the ship sent him?

The bear turned to worry at the arrow. Carefully, I explored the noose around her leg with my fingers. I picked at it until it began to loosen. I slipped the end of the rope through the noose and then carefully untangled rope and reeds from bear's fur and teased them away from where they had lodged within her skin. I flung the trapline hard into a clump of long grasses.

There!

She looked at me. Gave a little grunt. It wasn't gratefulness, exactly, but more like recognition: *I see that you have done this for me.* She began to lick her leg.

The arrow, I saw, wobbled a bit; maybe it had begun to work its way out. But the skin at its base was swollen and warm to the touch. *Festering*. Before, I had feared to pull it free, but now a hot surge of rage swept through me, and I had the knife from my belt before I knew it. I pressed the tip hard against the skin near the arrow-head, jiggled the shaft, and it was out. The bear's head jerked up; she let out a roar. I jumped back, away from her. She studied me for a long moment, then began to lick the arrow wound.

I let out my breath. Flung the arrow into the grass beside the rope.

But I wasn't finished. Not yet.

I slipped the knife under the harness at the bear's neck and sliced it through. Then I cut through the leather strip at her back. I caught the harness before it slid to the ground and threw it into the grass beside the rope and the arrow.

I was stealing, I knew. Stealing from the king.

So be it.

The bear was gazing at me again. I knew she was just a beast and had little understanding, but in that moment, it seemed that she knew well that an event of great gravity had just befallen her, something that would alter her life and mine.

She leaned toward me. Snuffled at my hair, my neck, my face.

"You're free now," I told her. "Where do you want to go?"

\\\\\\

As it happened, she wanted to go east.

She rested for a while by the edge of the bay and then dragged herself heavily to her feet, put her nose to the wind, and began to limp across the grassy meadow. No longer did she move with that majestic, galumphing grace I had loved to behold. She moved in a tentative, wounded way. Like prey.

This time, I followed *her*. I spared a glance to the north, in the direction of the village. I halfway hoped to catch sight of the *Queen Margrete*, but the sputtering rain made a dim gray screen all around us, and I could make out only a small stretch of the bay. My damp cloak and tunic clung to me; my feet chafed and stung. I tried not to think about a good, hot meal and a dry bed. I tried not to think about the doctor, for I knew in my heart he would be worried about me.

The ground grew ever soggier. The bear's footprints filled with water—and so did mine. It would take the trapper many hours to skirt the edge of the bay; if we were lucky, the rain would flood our tracks entirely.

We slogged along steadily, over ground veined with runnelling creeks and streams. We startled frogs from their perches, caused herons to take flight, and scattered rafts of paddling ducks. From time to time I saw the whiplash of a water snake slithering past. Clouds of biting insects buzzed about us, causing the bear to shake her head in vexation and raising itchy red welts on my skin.

I kept looking for the trapper, but saw no sign of him.

We continued east, toward the land of the Danes. I recalled seeing that coastline from the ship—a peninsula pointing north. . . .

To Norway.

Could the bear smell Norway on the wind? Could she feel the tug of home, like a migrating bird?

In the *Queen Margrete*, we had sailed past the gap between Norway and Denmark. The two lands had seemed a long way apart. . . but surely there must be islands in between? The bear was a powerful swimmer. Maybe she could ferry from one island to another. When winter came, the sea ice would draw the islands closer, and she wouldn't have to swim so far.

And as for me . . .

The bear and I would have to part company, in time. For a while I had reveled in my freedom, but now I longed for shelter and warmth and a good cooked meal.

And it came to me that bears can be free entirely, but men, unless they are kings, must bend a knee to someone. Even in Wales, I would have a master. And, truth be told, I craved the company of other people. My mother most of all, and the doctor . . . but even my stepbrothers would be welcome to me now. Even my stepfather. Even Hauk.

So, maybe I could find a nearby town or a village where I could overwinter. And after that . . .

Would my Welsh family accept me without the letter?

Would I ever see the doctor again?

And Mama . . . Would my stepfather allow me to return? If he did, could I stand to live by his rules, under his roof?

I put my head down and kept walking. I could no more see my future than I could see Norway, or even the *Queen Margrete*.

⇥ CHAPTER 38 ⇤

Pale, Soft Blossom

THE NEXT MORNING, the bear was gone. Shivering, I rose to my feet and looked about me. The rain had ceased at last; the sun peeked over the eastern horizon, and a sheer mist lay low over the bog. From the knoll on which we had slept, a new trail of mashed grasses thrust northward, toward the sea. I scanned the marsh, and there, in the distance, saw the long white limping shape of her cresting a small rise.

Why north? Why suddenly north, instead of east?

A heavy, sick feeling came to squat in the pit of my stomach. The bear had changed direction before, when . . .

And then I was running, running north, sloshing through marsh water, sinking into the mud, stumbling on rocks and roots. I called out to the bear to halt, to wait for me, but she did not, and soon she disappeared over the top of the hill.

I ran until my legs cramped with pain, until my breath tore ragged at my throat. By the time I crested the rise, most of the mist had burned off. At a distance lay the sea. Nearer: a river, and a cluster of small boats. Nearer still: the bear, surrounded by a ring of men. I heard shouting now, and the clash of metal.

The ring tightened about the bear, and all at once the air above her filled with nets—a pale, soft blossom, bursting and then collapsing upon her. And the running thrum took possession of me, and I was shouting at the top of my lungs. A lone figure came jogging toward me; he called my name and tried to take my arm when at last he drew near. I veered away from him—I *had* to reach the bear—but the doctor clasped his strong arms about me and said, "Stop, Arthur, stop, my son, stop, just stop, please, stop."

PART IV

LONDON

≋ CHAPTER 39 ≋

Betrayal

THEY STRIPPED ME of the knife and my belt and locked me in the unlit storeroom of the *Queen Margrete*. Soon I heard the sounds of the bear being loaded onto the ship—her roars of pain and rage and perplexity. I beat on the door until my knuckles bled. I begged to be with her, to be allowed to try to calm her. I called out for the doctor, but he never came.

"My son," he had called me.

What a sham!

After a while the sounds of the bear subsided, with only an occasional rumble of protest.

Now we were both of us prisoners.

I slumped down on the boards. What must *she* think of what had befallen her? The trap, the men, the noise, the cage, the return to the ship. Did she think that I'd had a hand in it? That I had betrayed her?

I told myself that I hadn't, and yet . . . I knew in my heart that until the past few days, I had plotted for her capture, as well.

And now what would happen to me?

It must be plain to the captain that I had conspired to let the bear go free. The bear who belonged to the king. So, would they return me to Norway to be tried for treason? Put me ashore on a deserted island? Hang me?

I waited, listening to the sailors' voices, to the various squeaks and knocks and clatterings of lading. In a while, after the movement of the ship told me that we were underway, I heard a clank of iron on iron outside the door. A foolish hope bloomed in my chest, but it wasn't the doctor, nor even Thorvald; it was a sailor I didn't know. He set down a bedroll and a bucket, lit the lantern that hung from the ceiling, then took his leave, locking the door behind him.

But later still, as I lay on the bedroll, the doctor came with a bowl of supper.

I turned my back to him. Some part of me was glad to have him near, but I didn't want to look at him. I didn't want to talk to him. I didn't want to listen to what he had to say.

He was supposed to care for the bear. Why hadn't he prevailed upon the captain to let me help with her? And he had allowed me to be imprisoned—just handed me over to the guards.

My son. Ha!

"Arthur," he said now. "Please eat."

The smell of roasted meat made the juices in my mouth gush like a spring. I had dreamed of a meal like this. But I didn't turn around.

"Arthur . . ." The doctor sighed, a sound that seemed to rise from somewhere deep inside him. I heard a rustling of cloth, and a thump, and I knew he had sat down beside me.

The ship rocked gently, in quiet seas. I heard the creak of the lines, a rumble of voices. I took a deep, long breath, and in the space of it recalled that it was the doctor who had persuaded the captain to take me on when I was destitute, and that I had pledged to help with the bear—not steal her away. I recalled that the doctor had had little choice but to obey the captain's orders, but that I had betrayed his trust of my own free will.

Presently, I heard the clunk of the bowl on the

deck, and I knew that the doctor was leaving. I longed to turn round, call to him not to go. But I couldn't. I heard the thump of the door as it shut behind him.

And I was alone again.

\\\\\

The second night, when the doctor came, I turned my back on him again, still unwilling to face him. But I smelled cod and bacon fat and fresh biscuits, and again my mouth began to water. I had devoured the previous night's supper after he had left, so I couldn't now feign to be so angry that I refused to eat. So when he offered me the bowl, I took it.

I sat cross-legged, and tucked in. The doctor lowered himself to the deck beside me and, as if betrayal did not hunker like a wolf between us, began to relate what had befallen him on the ship.

He had, he said, come looking for me during the storm. When he found the bear cage open, he had searched for both of us, but at last had to abandon ship. The following day, when storm and tide had ebbed, the *Queen Margrete* stood high and dry. She had not cracked up on a rocky shoal but had gone aground on the sandy shore of a coastal island. She was not badly damaged after all; they made temporary repairs in a few days and soon refloated her.

Meanwhile, they had sent out men to look for me—and for the bear. The doctor had gone himself, but a thick fog had settled in, making the search difficult. They had combed the island from one end to another, to no avail. After that, they had searched parts of the mainland as well, but had found no trace of us. Then some few of the sailors, seeking provisions at a village on the mainland, heard rumors about a boy and a large, pale bear.

"Then I knew you were alive," the doctor said, "or at least, that you had survived the wreck. Whether you would continue to survive the bear . . ."

The doctor's voice went to gravel; he cleared his throat.

I glanced up from my supper and, for the first time, caught his eye. I quickly looked away.

"*That*, I did not know," he concluded.

I picked up a chunk of cod and stuffed it into my mouth. I chewed. I swallowed.

"The trapper," the doctor began.

"You didn't send him to find *me*," I said. "Don't pretend you did. You sent the trapper to catch the bear."

The doctor said nothing. Then, "Arthur . . ."

His voice was so tender, I couldn't abide it. I stood, and the bowl went clattering to the floor. I lurched away from him and faced the wall. The ship rocked gently beneath my feet. The lantern cast shifting shadows across the timbers.

In a moment, the doctor went on, as if nothing had happened. The captain had hired the trapper, he said. The ship had limped east, to a port town the captain knew of, to finish repairs and to resupply. After I cut the bear from the noose, the trapper had rowed across the bay in a small boat he had stowed by the shore.

"He told us where you had been and in what direction you were bound. So," the doctor said, "we set the second trap." He paused, and then went on. "Arthur, she would never have reached Norway. It's too far to swim, even with the sea ice in winter."

Someway, I had known that, even though I had tried to believe she might make the journey home. Now I heard the snap of the sail above, and the creaking of lines. Outside the storeroom, one of the sailors broke into a mournful song. I turned to glance at the doctor. He was gazing into the shadows, seeming lost in his own thoughts. There was a gaunt look about him that I had not marked before.

He had gone searching for me, in the storm, and after. He knew I had released the bear and had not tried to return her to the ship, but he had not scolded me, nor even reproached me. Before, he had taken time to teach me, seeming to value me both for what I could do at present and for what I might learn to do in time.

It seemed that all the weariness in the world had gathered in the chambers behind my brow, in the acreage between my shoulder blades. I wanted to lie down. I wanted to close my eyes.

But I knew that I could choose to be a child and continue to spite him with my turned back . . . or I could be a man and look him in the eye.

I squatted down before him and gazed full into his face. He blinked, seemingly startled, and then his eyes crinkled at the corners—a warming of his countenance yet too sad to be called a smile.

"What will become of me?" I asked.

"The captain is fuming now, but he'll cool down soon enough. He'll need you when we reach London, and, after that . . . My guess is he'll let you go."

Let me go. So I would be free. Free, at least, to choose whether to bind myself to the Welsh princes, or to my stepfather, or to some other master.

"What will become of *her*?" I asked.

"She belongs to the king," the doctor said, not asking whom I meant. "Once we've turned her over to his protection, we may never hear word of her again, but we can trust that she'll be well cared for."

Again, I tried to imagine what the bear must be thinking about what had befallen her—and about my part in it. But a single word—*betrayal*—pierced me so violently and hard, I had to hold my chest with both hands to keep my heart from splitting.

"Will she ever be free?"

"No," the doctor said softly. "That, she will not."

CHAPTER 40

A Cartload of Trouble

THE DOCTOR, AS it happened, was right about the captain. He let me bide my time in the storeroom for a week or so until the last of the repairs were finished, and then we set sail for London. Some days later the seas went dead calm, and the shouts and thumps and scrapes and creaks and footfalls welled up in a clamorous wave, and I knew that we had come in to port. Soon, I heard the grate of a key in the lock, and the doctor stood before me, holding my belt and my boots. "Put these on," he said, "and be quick about it. Captain's released you to pacify the bear."

But my boots no longer fit. Either my feet were

yet swollen, or they had grown, or the callouses had layered over them too thickly. So I left my old boots behind.

The bear was pacing, hunched and taut, and I could see from her gait that her wounded rear leg still pained her. And yet she was magnificent. The bloodstains had gone from the fur near her arrow wounds and from her leg. Someone must have showered her with bucketsful of water, for she was all-over clean and even whiter than I had remembered. The raw size of her, to which I had accustomed myself on our sojourn, struck me with renewed force.

As I approached, she lifted her nose in the air, then swiveled her great head in my direction. She made a sound, then—a sound I cannot describe, a sound so filled with surprise and longing that for a moment, the world blurred before my eyes, and I had to duck my head.

I drew near to the cage, and the quivering black snout stretched out to me, sniffing at my eyes, sniffing at my cheeks, sniffing at my neck and shoulders and belly. I reached both arms through the bars and dug my fingers deep into the fur behind her ears, all the way down to the skin.

"Arthur," the doctor said.

I swallowed. Drew back from the cage and looked about me. The crew, I saw, was silent; many had turned from their work to stare. Thorvald nodded. Hauk scowled. Ottar, to my astonishment, gave me a quick, small smile and then dropped his gaze to the deck.

The doctor jerked his head, signaling me to look directly behind me.

The captain.

I straightened.

"I don't want any missteps with the bear on shore," the captain barked at me. "If she slams herself too hard against the bars, the cart could tip over, and that would be indecorous, to say the least. Your job is to keep her peaceable, do you hear me?"

"Yes, sir."

"There will be a procession through town, and she's to be passed in review before the king. Don't go within the cage—the bear's the attraction—not you."

One word snagged at me. The *king*?

"Arthur! Do you ken me?"

"Yes, sir."

The bear was to pass in review before the English king?

"Very well," the captain said. "Stay beside her up to the Tower of London gates, but don't go in. The bear will be Henry's problem then, and welcome to it!" The captain paused for a moment, and then in an easier tone, said, "You're not planning on escaping with her again, are you? Traipsing all over London? Maybe crossing the great bridge, the two of you rogues together, or wreaking havoc in the fish market, or claiming sanctuary in the cathedral?"

The captain cracked a smile. A wave of uneasy laughter coursed through the men.

"No, sir," I said.

"Very well, then," the captain said. "Your friends . . ." He cocked a wiry eyebrow in the direction of the doctor and at Thorvald beside him. "Your friends have been petitioning on your behalf. Without them, you'd be in a cartload of trouble. And you might be yet, if you don't do as I command. If I'm satisfied, I'll release you into the doctor's custody, and then I wash my hands of you!"

CHAPTER 41

Birthright

AFTER THAT, IT was as if a brisk, blustery wind had come upon us, for the air filled with shouting and creaking and clanking, and men swarmed all across the ship, and I had to cling to a corner of the bear's cage to avoid being jostled and swept off my feet and maybe trodden underfoot. A crane appeared overhead, and some intrepid sailor climbed to the top of the cage and set the hook.

I held my breath as the cage lifted off the deck and rose into the air above us, tilting and twisting. The bear slid from side to side, bellowing, scrabbling with her great feet and thudding against the bars, and a well of pity opened up in my heart. At last, the crane arm came to hover over a large, flatbed cart on the quay. Four men tied ropes to the cage, and amidst much shouting and maneuvering, the cage dropped onto the cart with a resounding thump.

I ran across the gangplank, dodging two sailors who were unloading cargo, their curses ringing in my ears. I made my way to the bear's cage and slipped between the bars. The bear snuffled at my face, my neck, my chest. I was murmuring to her, trying to comfort her, stroking the wide, flat space between her eyes, when an angry, honking cry sounded behind me. I turned to see a tall man dressed in King Haakon's livery. He had a long, pale, equine face, and hair so blond it was almost white. He stabbed an indignant finger in my direction and went on in that honking voice of his—something about an outrage, something about a disgrace, something about a sordid, tattered urchin, by which it was clear that he meant me.

The captain appeared beside him and spoke in a placating tone. I couldn't hear what he said, but soon the horse-faced man bleated out something to a servant, who disappeared into the crowd and reappeared before long with an armful of clothing. Horse Face motioned the servant toward me; the captain said,

"Arthur, put those on! And don't dawdle!"

And so I had to leave the cage, and strip off my clothes before the captain and the horse-faced man and God and everyone, and don the tunic and cloak and cap and stockings, which were of a finer, softer wool than any I had felt in all my life. And boots! Fine, supple leather boots, which were nonetheless too big for my feet. And all the while the captain was reminding me that I must walk beside the cage but not go within, that I was not to draw notice from the bear, for nobody had come to see *me*. He told me that King Haakon's envoy (the horse-faced man) would precede us along the route through the streets, and that when we came to the English king, I was to bow low, then stand aside and say nothing, not a single word, upon pain of death.

And then there was a commotion with a horse—a fine, white steed; a horse fit for a king—which was charged with pulling the bear's cart. Except this horse took one look at the bear, and then his eyes rolled back in his head, and he began to plunge and kick and whinny. Presently, an ox was brought out to do the job, which displeased the envoy exceedingly because he did not deem the ox fine enough to represent King Haakon—he judged it a disgrace—but the bear must be pulled by something, and so the ox it was.

At last, we set off through the streets of London. The sun had crested noon on this balmy, summer's day, and many folk came into the streets to watch. Soon, we formed ourselves into a procession, with the envoy going first, and a small contingent of Norwegian guards, and then a larger force of English guards, and then the ox, and then the bear, with the doctor walking to one side of her, and I to the other. Fine shops and inns and houses rose steeply to either side, but the streets themselves churned with mud and refuse, and before long my new boots looked as if I had been working all day in the fields like a peasant farmer. The procession grew as we went, adding on behind: a juggler, a small troupe of musicians, a stilt walker, and three acrobats who could turn cartwheels and walk on their hands. And yet, as we passed, all eyes were on the bear.

I think they would have liked her to be ferocious. Mothers clutched small children's hands, pulling them away from the cage. A drunkard stumbled beside us for a while, miming fear and horror. A troop of ragtag boys trotted alongside, snarling and growling at the bear, as if exhorting her to behave as a bear ought. One of them prodded her with a stick, no doubt hoping for a savage snap of teeth, or spine-tingling roar, or a delicious jolt of terror if the bear lunged against the bars of her cage. I guessed that some of the spectators wouldn't have minded if she broke out of her cage altogether and mauled a drunkard or two before she was recaptured.

And I, too, expected the bear to become skittish— at the very least, to pace in her restless way. I expected to feel the familiar running thrum in her. I thought she might snap at the boy with the stick; I thought she might swat a paw at the wretched drunkard. I feared that the captain might deem I had made a poor job of pacifying her; he might lock me up again.

But a strange sort of calm had come over her. While the whole human pageant strutted and whooped, she held herself with grave dignity. Did she sense that forces she didn't understand had overtaken her; that life had finally closed in and trapped her; that it was useless to protest?

Perhaps.

But as I watched her, the clamor all about me seemed to grow dim. In my mind's eye, I saw the stillness of a pale Norwegian sky in the moments before snowfall. The bright pulse of the aurora in the hush of night. I heard the silent ringing of the stars in their northern circuits, and the squeak of ice beneath my boots. I saw the flicker of moving water inside a frozen cascade; I caught the clean, mineral scent of ancient frost.

And now, as I gazed at her, the bear seemed to grow even larger in my imagination. Not just the solid bulk of her, but large in another way—large enough to hold all of it, all of the land that was her birthright, within her skin and bones and blood.

CHAPTER 42

Old Enemy

SOON, THE HOUSES and shops fell away to either side. We passed out of the town and into a wide meadow, toward a tall, gleaming-white tower surrounded by castle walls and a moat.

The captain had said *Tower of London*. That must be where the bear was bound.

As we drew near, I saw that part of the outer castle wall before us—the western wall—had collapsed into heaps of stony rubble that spilled into the moat. Workmen swarmed like bees over a latticework of wooden scaffolding set against the sections of wall that yet remained.

Just outside the moat stood a broad pavilion striped in orange and yellow and aflutter with festive banners. At first it seemed to me as if there was a garden within the pavilion—masses of reds and blues and browns and greens, shifting like blossoms in a gentle breeze. But before long the blossoms took on the shapes of gowns and robes and capes, and soon, I could make out the faces of the elegant lords and ladies who wore them.

And now one figure detached himself from the rest and strode out to greet us. He gave a great, loud bark of a laugh and called back to someone in the pavilion. A fur-lined purple cloak streamed from his shoulders, and many fine rings glittered on his fingers, and a golden circlet sat upon his brow.

Henry. The English king.

He held up a hand, motioning for us to halt.

Shouts rang out. Ahead, the Norwegian soldiers bunched up and came to a ragged halt. But the ox was slower to obey; he nearly plowed into the English soldiers, scattering them in disarray. The envoy shot out of the turmoil and went to bow before the king. They exchanged words I could not make out, and then both of them—the envoy and the king—made their way back toward the bear. Toward the doctor and me.

The doctor doffed his cap and bowed, and I did

too. The king halted so near, I could have taken two steps, reached out my hand, and touched the fur on his royal purple cloak.

My father's old enemy, the English king.

I was glad that the bear remained calm, her great black nose exploring, as if to seek out scents hidden in folds and crevices of air. I was glad of my new, fine raiment, for it would have been unseemly to stand two steps from the King of England in the dirt-and-blood, dung-and-sweat–stained garb that had served me all the way from Norway. I wondered what my mother would think if she could see me now, bowing before King Henry.

But the war with England had never been her fight, and it had ended not long after my father died. She would likely be grateful simply to know that I yet lived.

The doctor straightened, and I did too. The envoy kept up a smooth stream of chatter in a tongue I did not know. The king was frowning. There was something odd about his face—one eyelid drooped, as if he was halfway attending to his kingly duties and halfway longing for sleep.

The king flicked an impatient hand, and even I understood he was signaling the envoy to cease with his nattering. The king drew closer to the bear; the envoy started to follow, but the king shook his head, and the envoy stayed behind.

And now, as Henry regarded the bear, his frown softened. His countenance grew thoughtful and grave. The bear ceased sniffing and slowly turned toward him. They regarded each other in silence.

I don't know if it was the eye, but all at once it seemed to me that the king looked sorrowful. There was something of *recognition* in his gaze. I recalled that somewhere I'd heard talk of Henry's troubles with his nobles, and it occurred to me to wonder . . . Might it be that the king, too, knew what it was to have life hem him in and trap him, blocking his will as surely as the bars of an iron cage? Might it be that even kings were not entirely free?

The bear let out a low, warning rumble.

The king, with a slight smile, nodded, as if to a foreign potentate of equal rank. Abruptly, he turned and strode back to the tent.

The procession started up again: The soldiers regrouped; the ox lumbered forward; the cartwheels creaked; the musicians strummed and tootled in fits and starts. The envoy scurried to the fore, as if to demonstrate that *he* was leading our little band. When we came to the narrow wooden bridge across the moat, the soldiers peeled off and formed a rank to our rear. Now it was only the envoy, the ox, the bear, the doctor, and me. Our footsteps thudded on the boards; the sounds of music and voices grew dim behind. We crossed the moat and came to the guards before the gate, a makeshift gate with heaps of fallen stones to either side. The cart squeaked to a halt.

The bear was sniffing, sniffing. She turned to me and grunted, as if to say, *What are we doing now, Arthur? Who are these people? What is this place?*

I moved to the cage, and she snuffled in my hair and licked my right ear, the one the arrow had grazed. She pressed her nose into my neck. I felt a raw, ragged crater opening deep in the pit of my heart. I began to squeeze between the bars, to be with her. But the envoy honked out an indignant protest, and the doctor set a hand on my shoulder and said, "Arthur." He said, "Son."

And the gate swung open, and the ox began to move, and the creaky wheels squeaked, and the bear raised her nose into the air to search for answers I could not give her. I watched as the old fortress swallowed them up: the ox, and then the bear.

The envoy, scowling, snatched the fine, new cloak from my shoulders. And then the gate slammed shut with a resounding thump, and she was gone.

CHAPTER 43

He Will Find No Defenders

I KEPT MY fine new tunic, cap, stockings, and boots. The envoy did not come for them, and the doctor said I had earned them, in any case. "You'll grow into those boots soon enough," he said. "You'll see." He bought me a cloak—not so fine as the one the envoy had lent me, but still very handsome, and warm.

We went to an inn, where the doctor fed us both—a rich pie filled with mutton and eels. Then he took a room for us—a small, dim chamber with two cots, a desk, and a low bench upon which he kept his chest of herbs and remedies.

But I couldn't stop thinking about the bear.

What would they feed her? Would they know to hum to her? Scratch behind her ears? Would she even let them come near her?

The doctor assured me that the king could provide better fare than ever the bear had on the ship. And surely he would find a keeper who had a way with animals, like me.

I told myself that she would do well enough without me. But when I recalled the comfort of her great, furry paw pressed up against my side, an aching engulfed me, and I selfishly hoped she'd never do that with another.

The doctor told me of his plans to take us to Wales. *Us*, for he had always wanted to see Wales, he said, and so would travel there long enough to see me settled.

I had nearly abandoned hope of Wales. The letter was gone, and the more I considered the matter, the more I doubted I could find kin and property there without a letter to show those who might guide me. And would they accept me as my father's son? Did I favor him, I wondered, beyond my coloring and size? Would they see his face in mine?

Still, at the mention of Wales, I felt old hopes buoy up, confusing me. I didn't quite know who I was anymore, nor where I belonged.

"But the letter . . . ," I said. "The shipwreck . . ."

The doctor held up a finger. "Wait," he said, and smiled. Then he opened his chest and pulled out a folded parchment, and I recognized the broken seal.

The letter!

"But . . . Hauk stole it," I said.

"Thorvald threatened him within an inch of his life, and Hauk showed where he'd hidden your letter. Then Thorvald returned it to me."

"But the shipwreck . . ."

"The ship went aground," the doctor said, "not under. Some things were ruined but others survived."

So Hauk, without intending it, had likely done me a boon. For if he hadn't stolen it, the letter might well have been ruined by flooding water in the storeroom when the ship went aground.

"Still, no one can read it," I said. "It's in Welsh, not Latin."

"Perhaps no one in Norway can read it, but Welshmen are thick upon the ground in London. You can understand Welsh, can't you? If it's read to you?"

I nodded, a flicker of hope kindling in me.

"So we'll seek out a Welshman who can read."

We found one the next day in an alehouse nearby.

He was not tall, and his hair and eyes were dark. Like me. They said he was popular with the ladies, and indeed, his features were remarkably well-favored, and I caught a roguish twinkle in his eye. His name, he said, was Llyn. He took a deep swig from the tankard at his elbow and then reached out a hand for the letter.

But I hesitated.

I had been so certain of what the letter must say, had staked so much upon it. But now, of a sudden, I began to wonder if I had been mistaken. What had led me to judge so surely that my Welsh kin wanted and needed me to come and claim my birthright? Was it only hope that had made me believe?

"Arthur?" the doctor said.

I gave Llyn the letter.

He unfolded it, leaned in close to the flickering lamp on the table before us, and passed a finger over the first couple of lines. Looking up, he grinned and spoke to me in Welsh. "Oh, aye," he said. "I can decipher this, easy as falling off a pony." He spread out the letter on the table and began to read.

"'To her dearest Signy, formerly wife of Morcan of Gwynedd; Lady Cadwyn, sister of Morcan, sends peace and greetings.'"

The names, familiar from long ago, jolted something within me. I felt a flush warm my face, and tingle of excitement. The doctor was looking at me, questioning. "The writer is my aunt, Cadwyn," I said. "She sends greetings to my mother, whose name is Signy. Morcan was my father."

Llyn read on:

"'You should know, my friend, that there is very great distress and immense sorrow in my heart.'"

I shifted on the bench. This boded ill.

"'I cannot ken what word you have had of Wales, but since the truce with England, the young princes have been squabbling among themselves, and at the same time holding fast to their rancor against the former defenders of David.'"

Such as my father. This boded even worse.

Llyn read on, elaborating upon the royal family's quarrel, and then: "'It is Henry I blame for this,'" he read. "'I . . .'" Llyn looked about him, as if he feared someone might hear. Four men had come to sit at the table nearest us, but they were drinking and laughing; they paid us no mind. "Your aunt says," Lyn continued in a softer voice, "'I revile him. I curse his name. For had Henry not stripped us of lands fairly won, there would be enough of land and titles to satisfy all of the young princes, and they would have neither inclination nor leisure for the bearing of old grudges.'"

"Well?" the doctor asked me.

"Ah," I said, not wanting to give voice to my fears, "it seems that my aunt bears little love for the King of England."

Llyn read on:

"'These years since you departed I have striven to hold Morcan's lands against the arrival of your son, Arthur, when he comes into his majority next year. But now two of the young princes have seized . . .'"

Llyn flicked me a quick glance and read silently on, frowning. A serving maid brushed past our table; shadows flickered across the parchment. "Uh, your aunt says . . ." Llyn made a funny little humming sound deep in his throat, clearly discomfited.

"What is it, son?" the doctor asked me. Upon receiving no reply, he turned to Llyn. "Read, man, what are you waiting for!"

Llyn didn't know Norse, but the doctor's meaning was clear. Llyn hoisted his tankard, drank deeply, and then continued:

"'. . . have seized Morcan's lands and there is naught to be done. With affairs standing as they are, I . . .'" Llyn's voice sank to a murmur, and I had to strain my ears to hear him over the rising din of talk and laughter. "'. . . I urge you not to send Arthur back to claim his birthright, for he will find no defenders and might provoke further retribution against me and my suffering daughters.'"

Llyn cleared his throat. He did not look up.

"Arthur, what is it?" the doctor asked.

. . . seized Morcan's lands . . .

. . . he will find no defenders . . .

. . . provoke further retribution against me and my suffering daughters . . .

They didn't want me.

It was true that I had had second thoughts about returning to Wales, but this—after all my dreams and imaginings, after leaving home and risking the long journey—this struck me like a mule kick to the chest.

Abruptly, I stood, face burning. The bench scraped and toppled behind me; I held out my hand for the letter.

"Arthur?" the doctor said.

Llyn looked uncertain. He did not relinquish the letter straightaway, but quickly scanned what was left and said, "There's a bit more about Welsh politics. Your aunt wishes that your mother and your kin may abide in peace and prosperity, and—"

"Give it to me," I said.

With a glance at the doctor, Llyn made a careful, silent production of folding the letter.

A burst of laughter arose from the next table. A burly man stumbled into ours; the ale sloshed from its tankards; the candlelight leaped. I took a deep breath of burning tallow and sour brew and sweat. Suddenly, I felt ill.

Llyn handed me the letter. "I'm sorry," he mumbled.

The doctor slipped him a couple of coins; I fled.

CHAPTER 44

Trouble with the Bear

OUTSIDE THE ALEHOUSE, I flung the accursed letter into the muddy verge and trod it underfoot, then set off through the streets of London. A fine rain was sifting down, and though I had intended to return to the inn, shame and disappointment burned hot within me, and I couldn't abide the thought of penning myself up in a dim, cramped room. I jostled a woman with a market basket on her arm; she shook her fist and scolded me. I dodged to avoid a black-robed friar and then plowed through a knot of gossiping fishermen when a hay cart blocked my path. Before long I caught a glimpse of the Tower looming above the rooftops ahead, and I knew I'd been yearning to go there all along.

By the time I reached the wooden bridge across the moat, my cloak was sodden and my fine new boots caked with mud. I jogged across, my footsteps loud and hollow. The gate loomed before me, with hillocks of rocky rubble stretching out to either side. Two guards flanked the gate, watching me.

My feet slowed, then stopped. "Bear!" I called.

One of the guards stepped forward.

"Bear!" I cried again. "Do you hear me, Bear?"

The guard was walking toward me, but I held my ground and strained my ears, for I felt that if I could only hear her—just one little grunt or snort from her—I would be able to turn back round and face whatever of life that must be faced. But there was only the crunch of the guard's feet on the gravel; there was only the chink of the stonemasons' chisels; there were only the men's voices in the bailey beyond the gate.

"Bear! Can you hear me?"

The guard halted a few steps before me. He said something in a gruff voice, and though I didn't know his language, I knew he was telling me to leave. And I would have obeyed, if I only could have heard her voice, just once.

"Bear!"

The guard lifted his pike and pointed it at me. He barked out something harsh. And then I heard footsteps behind me, and there was the doctor, running hard and out of breath. He commenced to speak in French; the guard, listening, lowered his pike. There was a colloquy back and forth between them, the doctor coming near me, taking my arm.

"Tell him I want to see her," I told the doctor. "Tell him I want to be sure they're caring for her properly."

"You can't see her, son," the doctor said. "She belongs to the king."

I pulled my arm away. "Don't call me *son*. I'm not your son! I had a father—a real father—and he loved me, and if he were alive, he would have wanted me beside him. He would have taught me to train the royal horses. We would have ridden with the princes to battle the enemies of Wales. We would have—"

Something broke inside me. My knees buckled, and a horrible, convulsive sound escaped my lips.

The guard raised his pike again, advanced upon us. The doctor had words with him in French and then turned to me.

"Arthur," he said, "let's go. There are things I need to say to you. Come. Come along back with me, please."

I listened again for the bear, but there was only the swish of grasses in the wind; there was only the bleak cry of a raven overhead. This time, I let the doctor take me by the arm and lead me back across the bridge.

"I had a son," he told me. "I had a wife."

We were back in our room again, each sitting on his own cot. A ray of late sunlight slipped through the shutters and lay a long, yellow ribbon upon the floor.

"They perished of the fever," the doctor said. "Both of them."

I looked up. The fever. Like my father.

"And after that," he said, "I never wanted . . . to lose another that way. And so with you, I resolved that it would be a practical alliance only, that I would serve your interests, and you mine. But when the ship went aground, and I thought I would never lay eyes on you again . . ."

He bowed his head, holding the bridge of his nose between thumb and forefinger.

I breathed in the quiet darkness of the room. The running thrum was entirely gone from my body, and just for this moment, I had no desire to be anywhere other than here, with this quiet, steady man.

"King Haakon has released me now," he said,

turning to me, "and I'm free to work where I please. I would like to return to Bergen. You could be my eyes for close-up work, and I could train you. Or, if you prefer, I could return you to your mother and stepfather."

"But you said you wanted to see Wales."

"Only because of you, Arthur. It's time to choose: Where do you want to go?"

I heard the echo of the question I had asked the bear after I had freed her from the noose. Her presence nearby still tugged at me hard, and I longed to be close.

But I knew I couldn't stay here alone. I had no means to earn room and board and couldn't even have speech with these Londoners. And the doctor, who had treated me more like a son than ever my stepfather had done . . . The doctor had offered me a safe home and secure living at a skilled trade. And I could see Mama again, and ease her mind.

So, I, like the bear, chose to return whence I had come. I told the doctor I would go to Norway to work with him, and I surely would have done so . . . if not for the knock at the door.

\\||//

It came a week later, after we had booked passage on a ship bound for Bergen.

The doctor pulled the door ajar and spoke to

someone in the hallway. Then he stepped aside, and a stranger entered our room.

He was tall and thin and knobby—knobby knees, knobby knuckles, knobby nose, knobby Adam's apple in his throat. I surmised from his dress that he was a bit of a dandy, with a fine red woollen cloak and matching cap, and boots worked in two colors of leather. He dipped his head in a small, friendly greeting as he spoke to the doctor in French. But his eyes sought past the doctor—sought *me*—his long, homely face creased with worry.

"Arthur," the doctor said, "here is William de Botton, who has been appointed by the king as keeper of his menagerie. He wishes to have words with you."

Why he would want to speak with me I could not begin to guess. And what was that word, *menagerie?*

The man seemed to read the puzzlement in my face, for he launched into a longish stretch of French, addressing the doctor and me, in turn.

"It seems," the doctor translated, "that a number of beasts are kept within the fortress of the Tower of London—not just the bear. Rare beasts—most, like the bear, gifts to the king from foreign rulers. Master de Botton heard about you from the guard at the gate, and he has searched you out."

The keeper turned and spoke directly to me. His look of worry deepened; he seemed to be making a plea. Though I could not comprehend a word of it, I knew, somehow, the gist of what he had to say.

There was trouble. Trouble with the bear.

CHAPTER 45

Master de Botton

WE HAD AN uneasy moment, then, as Master de Botton plainly wished to stay and have speech with us for a time, and there was no proper place for him to sit. But the doctor bade him come within, removing the medicine chest from the bench and gesturing for the keeper to take it. We perched on a cot, the doctor and I, and fixed our eyes upon the keeper.

He put me in mind of a grasshopper, with his bony legs thrusting up well above the seat, one leg jiggling with pent-up energy. He was not as old as the doctor—maybe three decades, rising four. His feet and hands were unusually large, like a puppy that has room to grow. And, despite his foppish garb, he smelled of animals—of hay and dung and fur.

He began to speak, and the doctor translated for me.

The bear was languishing. She did not eat, she did not pace, she did not roar. She lay on the floor of her cage with her eyes dully open, but neither groomed herself, nor lifted her nose to sniff the air, nor paid heed to the world about her. The keeper had seen this down-in-the-midden temper before in captive creatures, and many of them, he said, did not survive it.

I felt the ragged hole open up in the pit of my heart again.

The keeper said he had heard that the bear and I shared some uncommon bond. I nodded. This was true, but . . .

I recalled her easy, galumphing grace, loping through the open meadows. I recalled her joyful romps through the marsh water, covering herself with mud. I recalled how she had plunged into a cold river and emerged with a flopping fish in her mouth. For a time, she had been free.

The keeper went on. He said that he had tried feeding her all manner of fish; he had tried even veal and pork. He had called on the envoy, who told him ice bears vastly prefer seals, and the keeper had sent out a hunter to trap one. But it hadn't yet arrived, and meanwhile, the bear continued to decline.

He stopped for a moment. Looked directly at me. When next he spoke, his tone was beseeching.

The doctor translated: "Master de Botton wishes to know what else you've seen her eat. Something else that he might try."

My hands wanted to move to my chest, to hold my heart together, but I forced them to stay in my lap. "It was only cod, on the ship. And I didn't have to feed her at all, when she was free. I saw her eat fish, and wild eggs, and berries." The doctor translated for the keeper again and then translated his reply for me:

"But when she was caged . . . How did you coax her to eat, then?"

"There was no need for coaxing," I said. "She ate of her own accord."

The keeper gazed at me. He attempted a smile, but it didn't take.

I turned to the doctor. "Tell him to hum to her. Tell him she likes to be scratched behind her ears. Tell him to dig his fingers deep, all the way to her skin."

The doctor gave me a skeptical look, but translated;

the keeper seemed startled to hear it. He asked something; the doctor answered and then turned back to
me. "The keeper is astonished that you were able to
touch her. He says the only time she shows signs of
life is when someone comes near, and then she growls
and snarls."

So she was alone in there, with no one to hum to
her or scratch her.

To my mortification, tears pricked at my eyes.

"Ah," the keeper said, and I needed no translation.
Then he leaned forward and asked me a question.

The doctor sighed, said nothing.

I tapped his arm. "What did he say?"

"Listen, Arthur, you can't bide here in London until
the bear decides to eat—it could be months; it could
be years; it could be never."

I felt a bright, slow current of hope rising within
me. "What did he *say?*"

"He asks . . ." The doctor hesitated. "Asks if you
would visit the bear to see if you can persuade her to
eat. But—"

"Yes!" I said. "Tell him yes!"

"I'll tell him," the doctor said, "that we will consider
the matter tonight and deliver our answer tomorrow at
the fortress gate."

\\\\//

After the keeper took his leave, the doctor admonished me.

"You've chosen to return to Norway, son—you can't let the bear rule your life."

"But no one else can help her."

"You heard what the keeper said. Some animals don't thrive in captivity, no matter what we do. Maybe it wasn't you, but the seafaring that quickened her appetite—we'll never know."

"Yes, but—"

"Arthur—listen to me! Who knows when we'll see another ship bound for Norway? You're a man now. You need to put a stake in the ground—find your place in the world and begin making your way in it."

"Don't you think I know that?" I protested. For so long I had craved to be *of consequence* in the world. There was no place for me on the steading, and I was denied my birthright in Wales. Now the doctor had offered me another path . . . but the bear needed me. She had stood my friend when I needed *her*, and after all we had been through together, I was bound to her in ways that nobody else could understand.

"She is the king's bear," I said. "Remember, you told me? A gift from King Haakon. You said if there's something amiss with her, it reflects badly on our king."

"But she's no longer in your charge," the doctor said.

"She is if I'm the only one who can rouse her to eat." And it struck me that the doctor was a poor one to be making this argument. For I was no longer in *his* official charge, and yet here he was—feeding me, clothing me, finding me passage to Norway, offering me a living—and paying for it all out of his own purse. And I knew it was no longer a matter of duty with him, but, as with the bear and me, a matter of the heart.

CHAPTER 46

The Menagerie

WE RETURNED TO the fortress the following day. The doctor stated our business to one of the guards, the one who had come at me with a pike. He scowled at me, but sent a courier to fetch Master de Botton nonetheless.

We waited. I began to pace, consumed by eagerness and dread. Would the bear be glad to see me? Or was her spirit so far broken that she wouldn't care?

All about me I heard the ringing of chisels on stone. Flecks of rock dust glinted in the air, and workers scuttled up and down the wooden scaffolding. The doctor had told me that the king had erected a gate turret in the center of the western wall a dozen or so years before. But the turret had collapsed suddenly, as if struck by a quaking of the earth, ruining all of the forebuildings and outworks, as well as the surrounding portions of the wall.

In a while the gate creaked open, and there stood Master de Botton, who seemed mightily glad to see us. He led us along a dirt path toward the great white tower, but soon veered to the right, into a small grove of fruit trees in the outer bailey.

I heard the menagerie before I saw it—a medley of shufflings, grunts, and growls. A high, eerie cry pierced the air, issuing from bird or beast, I could not tell. And now came a roar, the likes of which I had never heard in all my days—an ancient, feral thunder of a roar, fathoms deep and dangerous—causing the hair on my head to prickle, and my knees to soften like wax.

Soon, it came into sight before me—a motley cluster of wood and iron cages set among the trees. I glimpsed a thatch of black fur in one, and the swish of a tufted tail in another, and a striped, doglike beast in a third. An outlandish, humpbacked creature, taller than a horse, stood chained and staked nearby.

There were more, but I did not stop to study

them, nor marvel at their strangeness. My eyes sought beyond, to an iron cage I knew well.

She was lying on the floor of it, legs splayed out behind, her great, pale head resting on a massive paw. As we neared, I saw her nose begin to twitch, and then her head lifted and turned toward me. She let out a soft grunt and clambered to her feet. And then I was running—running past the striped dog, past the humpbacked beast. I heard the doctor call "Arthur!" but I paid him no mind. I slipped between the bars of the cage and wrapped my arms about her long, soft neck . . . and then I knew beyond the ghost of a doubt that Norway would have to wait.

CHAPTER 47

A Heart Can Be Broken

BUT SOMETHING WAS still amiss.

Over the next few days I coaxed the bear to eat a little. Bits of salmon, a nibble of trout, a few scraps of beef and pork. But even when I hand-fed her while sitting at her side, it wasn't enough. I knew how much she ought to be eating. On the ship, she had wolfed down bucketsful of cod.

She no longer paced restlessly to and fro in her cage, and I couldn't feel the hum of the running energy on her. She took small interest in her surroundings, staring dully into the far distance. Sometimes I could cheer her by humming to her and scratching behind her ears, at which she groaned with pleasure and snuffled my hair and neck.

Recalling what I had told him about the bear's forage in the Low Countries, the keeper brought her three or four kinds of eggs and some blackberries. The bear lipped each berry from my hand and swallowed it. But she turned up her nose at the eggs.

I asked the doctor to tell about the rabbit haunch she had eaten in the warehouse in Bergen, and the next day the keeper produced a rabbit broiled to perfection. I held it out to her. She sniffed at it, but only nibbled at a bit of its skin. "Eat, Bear!" I pleaded. "Don't be a dunderhead—*eat!*"

As the days rolled by, the keeper produced a diversity of food for her. A lamb. A fox. A goose. While she sometimes showed interest, she never ate more than a few bites.

From time to time the doctor and the keeper put their heads together for long, worried colloquies. I heard the word *leopard* often when they spoke, and I asked the doctor about it. He seemed loathe to tell me, but finally relented. It seemed that Emperor Frederick had given King Henry three leopards some years before. They had lost interest in their food, and in behaving as leopards do.

"And how did it fall out for them?" I asked.

The doctor hesitated. Then: "One at a time, over several years, they died."

Died. The word struck a knell, deep at the center of me.

I had thought that if I could stay with the bear at least part of every day, she would recover her spirits. I had thought she needed *me*—that I would be enough for her, that I could heal her heart. But a heart can be broken in many different ways. A heart can be broken when you yearn for home, or when you're denied the life you were born to. A heart can be broken by a cage.

And what of my heart, if she refused to eat? How would I live, if she didn't?

The keeper told the doctor that the seal hunter ought to be back soon. He said that ice bears often fasted for months at a time when the sea ice broke up and they couldn't catch seals.

I knew very well how my bear loved the taste of seal. She had sacrificed her freedom for it.

And so I pinned all my hopes upon the seal hunter's return.

\\\\//

The bear slept during the heat of the day, and often, as she did so, I helped the keeper feed the other

animals in the menagerie. There was a lynx, familiar from home in Norway—and two other cats that
were frightfully large and fierce and strange. One was
sleek and black; another, tawny brown with a great
wide mane. There was the menacing, striped, doglike
beast; and the long-necked, humpbacked horse I had
marked before. There was a small, waddling creature
clothed in black-and-white quills that rattled when it
moved; and a lamb-sized, jewel-blue bird that called
out like a startled child and fanned its splendid tail
feathers in a brilliant and quivering screen.

These creatures too had been torn from their
homelands and confined in cages, and yet they ate
and seemed to prosper. The next time the doctor came
to the menagerie, I asked him to inquire of Master de
Botton about this.

The keeper turned and regarded me gravely as he
comprehended what the doctor was saying. When he
answered he spoke directly to me, as he was wont to
do when answering my questions, even though I could
understand but few of his words.

"He says he doesn't know," the doctor translated,
"why one animal thrives and another does not. He
deems it may be too cold here for some, and it may be
too warm for your bear. He says the food here is not

what they would eat in their own lands, and perhaps it does not suit them—"

The keeper interrupted to say something more; the doctor listened.

"He says he thinks that some wild creatures, like some people, can't get past mourning what they have lost."

A matter of the heart.

I nodded to the keeper to show him I understood. I knew it might seem strange, to some, to think that mere beasts might be capable of mourning. But I had lived on a farm for many years. I had seen a ewe bleating for hours over the body of her dead lamb, and a dog moping for weeks after the death of his littermate. Again, I wondered: Was the bear a mother? Did she mourn for her cubs?

This pricked me in a familiar, sore place. Mama. I couldn't return to her now, and didn't know if ever I would. But it was past time for me to try to put her mind at ease.

That evening, after supper, I asked the doctor if he would take down a letter.

"For whom?" he asked.

"My mother. To tell her that I am well."

\\\\\

Though the doctor had planned to return to Bergen, he let the ship sail without him. We moved from our chambers in the inn to a small room above a cobbler's shop, and the doctor began treating patients. In the evenings we supped together at an alehouse nearby. And afterward he began teaching me bits of French, for that was what the keeper and most of the fine folk in this place spoke, and the doctor was as ignorant of English as I.

Every day I returned to the fortress, to the bear. I had never laid eyes on the king or his court since that first time; the doctor told me that the king had many castles and stayed at the Tower but rarely.

And then one day the keeper appeared from the direction of the water gate, pushing a cart and calling my name. The seal!

Such a small, gray, sad, dead thing. Together we heaved the seal into the bear's cage and shut the door.

The bear raised her nose to taste the air, as if some faint memory had wafted in on a breeze. Slowly, she heaved herself to her feet. She put her nose down to the seal and sniffed. Then she turned aside and lay back down again.

The keeper bowed his head.

I slipped through the cage bars, dug my fingers into her fur, and shook her. "Eat!" I said. "It's a seal—don't you see?"

She heaved out a deep, groaning sigh, but didn't move.

≡ CHAPTER 48 ≡

The Parcel

OVER THE NEXT few weeks, as summer waned, a heavy sickness came to live in my belly and wouldn't go away. Though the bear's new fur had grown in after the molt—white as a baby's first tooth—it soon grew dingy and began to hang loose on her. Clouds of flies came to buzz round her head, and she didn't stir herself to swat at them. Her eyes grew sunken and crusty. I pleaded with her to eat, held one morsel of food after another in front of her nose. Sometimes she ate a little. But her heart wasn't in it . . . and it wasn't enough.

Often, I recalled what the captain had said about the bear and me making our escape and traipsing through

London. It had been a jest, but still . . . I imagined coming to her at night, unlocking her cage, and setting her free. Together, we would wend through the dark streets, ducking around corners to avoid passersby, and standing still—perfectly still—when the night watchman hove into view. We would wait until he passed, then make our way east through the city, leaning into the shadows and whispering our feet against the ground. After a time the bear would lift up her nose, stretching to taste a stray breeze from the North Sea. Then she would veer toward the river delta, hastening her steps. She would slip into the water and strike out swimming for home.

It was a whimsy—only a wish. But I drew brief comfort from imagining her escape, and it was better by far than facing up to the fate that awaited her.

\\\\//

One day in September, a courier arrived at our door. The doctor spoke with him in French for a few moments, and then the courier handed me a parcel wrapped in burlap.

"What is this?" I asked.

"Someone gave it to the captain of the *Queen Margrete*, asking that it be delivered to 'the one who tended the ice bear,'" the doctor said. "The captain commissioned this man to find you."

The doctor gave the courier a coin; he left. I bore the parcel to the window, where a wash of pale, late-afternoon light seeped into the room.

"Open it," the doctor said.

I did.

It held two objects, each swaddled in a clean, soft rag. When I unwrapped the first, I knew it at once.

My spoon case.

Carefully, I prized it open.

My spoon.

"Yours?" the doctor asked.

I nodded.

They were like old friends, the spoon and its case— so fitting to my hand. I reached for the other wrapped object and found a smooth, rounded chunk of wood.

A carving.

A bear.

I would have known her anywhere. Her long neck; her pigeon-toed front feet. The arrow scar on her shoulder. Her small, rounded ears. Her patrician nose, held up to the air and sniffing, as if mapping the dimensions of her world.

It was finely done, the carving, with many tiny features, down to the harness spanning the bear's neck and upper back.

And here, a scrap of parchment with words on it, writ large. I gave it to the doctor. He brought it up near his face, squinted, blinked. He read aloud:

> Dung Boy.
> Sorry.
> Ottar.

Why?

I remembered the quick smile Ottar had given me after I was reunited with the bear. Because I hadn't hit him? Because I had protected him from Thorvald?

Who could know?

I traced a finger across the surface of the wood, following the thin, raised line of the harness. I recalled how I had buckled it that first time in the warehouse; how I had held on to it as the bear ferried me ashore after the *Queen Margrete* ran aground; how I had sliced through the leather to free the bear in the end. I had fancied that I was releasing her from the emblem of her bondage, but instead, I had delivered her to another cage.

I clasped the carving in my hand, feeling the old energy thrumming in my blood, and an idea began to take shape in my mind.

CHAPTER 49

Fourteen Different
Kinds of Havoc

I TOLD MYSELF not to raise my hopes too far, that it was a fanciful plan with only a sliver of hope of success. But a kind of fire had begun to burn within me, and it persisted no matter how I tried to damp it.

And so, the next afternoon, I left the menagerie earlier than usual. I made my way west through the streets of London until I beheld the great stone bridge across the River Thames—a bridge unlike any I had seen before, a bridge that looked like a city street lined on either side with shops and houses. I found my way onto it, jostling against friars and fishwives, merchants and beggars, and packs of roving dogs. I veered to dodge a clattering donkey cart filled with turnips and onions, ducked between two pilgrims on ponies, and flattened myself against a wall to avoid a flock of bleating sheep. I passed a lute-strumming minstrel, a spice monger hawking his fragrant wares, and a man who shoveled animal dung from the street.

On the far side of the Thames, I headed back eastward. In the gaps between the warehouses on the riverfront, I saw ships sailing upstream and down, and fishing boats bobbing on the waves, and smaller craft darting in and out, ferrying folk from one side of the river to the other.

I walked down to the sand-and-grass verge of the Thames, directly across from the white tower. From here I could see the southern castle wall, and the roofs of the smaller towers in the inner ward, where king and company stayed when at the fortress. The riverbank—a long, thin strip of sand with a stout wooden pier—lay just outside the wall. The water gate, with its iron portcullis, created a narrow passage from the riverbank to the outer bailey—not far from the menagerie itself.

Yes. It might be possible.

I knelt, and swished my hand in the water. It was cold, but not so cold as it might be. Summer was passing, but the river yet held its heat.

So much about my idea seemed doubtful. Doubtful that it would work at all; doubtful that those in power would allow me to try. I would have to persuade the doctor first, tonight. And if I managed that, I would have to persuade the keeper, and he would have to persuade a string of men above him, and the more I thought of *them*, the more the word *impossible* slipped in and dragged at me.

But still . . .

The bear was dying. That was clear. And I had done all within my power to keep her alive, except for this one last thing.

\\\|//

"Swim?" the doctor said. "In the river? Arthur, you know they won't let her—"

"Wait, I haven't yet told you—"

"Why, she would just swim away," the doctor said, "wouldn't she? And then she would climb ashore somewhere in the city and wreak fourteen different kinds of havoc. We would have to capture her again, and the Lord only knows what they would do to her then." He rose, scraping the stool on the floor behind him, and began to pace the floor.

"There would be a harness," I said. "And a long, strong rope that would be staked to the ground or made fast to the portcullis."

"And how would we convey her from her cage to the river?" he demanded. "Tell me that. Because they won't go to the trouble of hoisting her cage onto a cart and hitching an ox to it once a month or once a week or whenever it suits the bear's fancy."

"Every day. She—"

"Every day! That's impossible, Arthur. And—"

"I'll lead her to the river. She'll follow. And two strong men with ropes could hold her, though we won't truly need them; she—"

He turned on one heel and stabbed a forefinger in my direction. "Two men couldn't hold her. Nor three, nor four. Did de Botton put this cockeyed notion into your head? God's truth, that man is consumed with his creatures; he treats them like nobility!"

"*I* thought of it. It's *my* notion. And I'm asking you . . . to translate for me when I tell it to the keeper."

"Listen, Arthur. I know the keeper is fond of you, but he's the king's man. Believe me, they'll put the bear's safety over yours. We can't trust them not to leave you in peril of your life. If the bear escapes, they'll use you as bait to get her back—"

"Do you mean they might make me lead the bear into her cage, all by myself, by leaving a trail of fish?"

The doctor stopped. He gazed at me for a moment

and then lowered himself onto his cot. He bowed his head and pinched the bridge of his nose between thumb and forefinger.

The hearth fire crackled and leaped, sending shadows across the room. I could hear a horse clop by outside, and voices. I halfway wished I could take back my words, but they had been gnawing at me for a good long while, and no force on Earth could unsay them.

When the doctor looked up, he spoke in a quiet voice. "I should have protected you then. I should never have allowed—" He shook his head. "I have rued it ever since."

I turned away. I knew I could make it easier for him. I could say that I had imperiled *myself* with the bear more than he had endangered me, which was true. I could say that the bear had never shown me the slightest danger or harm, which was also true. I could say that the doctor had protected me and aided me over and over since that time. True again. And that I knew that for quite some while he had loved me as a son.

But he *had* put me in harm's way, that once. And for my purposes now, I couldn't hold him blameless.

"After all that's passed," I said, "I owe the bear *my* protection. Maybe I can do nothing for her, but I have to try. Do you see? And if you love me—"

"Arthur—"

"If you love me, you will help."

Something moved in the doctor's throat. He gazed at me for a long moment, and then he said, "I do and I will, my son."

"Swim?" the keeper said. "In the river? Arthur, you know I can't permit . . ."

With the doctor translating all the while, the keeper raised many of the same objections I had heard from the doctor. That the bear might not have the will to escape, but nobody could hold her at the end of a rope if she did. That she could fetch up somewhere in London, causing injury to herself and others and creating no end of trouble for us all. That the keeper would have to send me to help bring her back, at much peril to myself. That she was a wild creature, and wild creatures were ever unpredictable.

But the keeper had seen firsthand the bond between the bear and me. And he knew how feeble she was—so she might more easily be restrained.

In the end he made me no promises. But neither did he refuse outright.

⟩ CHAPTER 50 ⟨

Le Roi

ON A FROSTY autumn day, the king and his party came to stay at the Tower. The entire fortress was now overrun with knights and squires, farriers and grooms, servants and maids and ladies-in-waiting. A week after they arrived, I looked up from cleaning the bear's cage and saw a messenger in royal livery striding past. He spoke briefly to the keeper, who seemed to grow taller as he listened. When the messenger had finished, the keeper brushed off his red cloak and straightened his cap. He glanced at me and said something to the messenger, who looked back at me, frowned, and shrugged.

The keeper called my name, pointing at my boots

with a flicking gesture. Then he walked a few steps backward, saying something in French, and made a large, scooping motion with one arm. He pivoted and set off with the messenger toward the gate to the inner ward.

I didn't understand a word the keeper said, and yet his meaning was clear:

Scrape your boots. Follow me.

\\\\/

We headed down the path toward the tower near the river where the king kept his residence. Two armored guards stepped aside at the doorway to admit the keeper and the messenger, but one of the guards moved to block my way.

The keeper spoke to him, lifting his chin in my direction.

The guard didn't move. He looked me up and down, taking in the grime on the hem of my cloak and the bits of filth I hadn't entirely scraped off my boots.

The messenger said something to the guard. It was not French he spoke, but the language of the common folk here.

The guard stepped aside.

The keeper gestured me to wait in the small, stone-lined anteroom just within the door. He flicked his hand toward my boots, and up a bit, silently bidding me to clean off the remaining muck. Then he followed the messenger through an arched doorway and up a spiral stone staircase.

I was alone.

A narrow stone bench stood against one wall, but I was too restless to sit. I brushed at my boots and cloak to little effect, soiling my hands in the process. I paced back and forth in the small chamber, as the bear used to do in her cage.

I was in the residence of the king. Maybe the keeper was telling Henry my idea—mine!—at this very moment. And the bear . . . Maybe there was a chance for her.

Would the king consider my plea? Would he grant leave to put it to a test?

Soon, I heard a commotion outside the door—voices, a clattering of footsteps. I heard the honking tones of the Norwegian envoy, sounding rushed and breathless, much displeased. He burst into the room, glared at me, and with two aides behind him, pounded up the spiral stairs.

I slumped onto the bench. If the king relied on *his* counsel, my plan was doomed. I sat for a while, but then the running thrum came into me again, jangling in my legs and arms, and I resumed my restless pacing.

After a while I heard more footsteps on the stairs. The keeper shot out of the archway. He plucked a piece of straw from my hair, scrubbed at a spot on my cloak, and then motioned me to turn around. I felt him brushing at my back, and when I had turned to face him again, he tossed a few more bits of straw to the floor and surveyed me with a frown. He motioned me to follow, and headed across the anteroom toward the stairs.

My legs would not obey. The keeper turned back and said something in a gentler tone than I had expected. I did not understand his words, of course, except for a single term that the doctor had taught me: *le roi*.

The king.

⪩ CHAPTER 51 ⪨

Tell Me Who You Are

SOMEHOW, I FOLLOWED the keeper up the stairs. My heart swelled to thrice its usual size and beat at the walls of my throat; the stone-cold air pressed against me like river water when you wade upstream. I heard a murmuring of voices—softer in the stone staircase, and then louder as we emerged.

A dim corridor.

An arched doorway ahead—streaming with light.

The keeper halted, set his hands on my shoulders, and gazed straight into my eyes. I couldn't decipher his look, for it seemed full of many contrary sentiments. Hope and pity. Solace and fear.

At last he turned, and we strode down the corridor together.

Two men-at-arms at the door moved aside to let us pass. I trailed behind the keeper and mimicked what he did: knelt and doffed my cap. Entered at a voiced command. Made my way across the wide stone floor.

At first, I couldn't find the king. Sunlight slanted in through a window just ahead, dazzling my eyes. To my left, rivers of colored light washed across the floor, and to my right, fire blazed in a wide hearth with bright-hued tapestries to either side. A knot of men stood in one corner of the room. Beyond them I saw the candlelit sconces; I saw the high, white throne; I saw the king, clad in scarlet and gold, upon it.

We moved toward him, and when we were near, the keeper knelt again, and so did I. The flames of a dozen flickering candles jumped as the king gestured for us to rise.

I remembered him from before—the halo of light brown hair; the golden circlet; the one odd, half-closed eye. He regarded me steadily, and I didn't know what to do with my own eyes, whether it would be better to look at him directly, or away. So I studied the rich fabric of his gown, below his knees—a thick velvet the color of rubies. I breathed in the smells of beeswax, of sweat, and of smoke.

The king spoke in French, and while I could not make out the meaning of what he said, I picked out my name among the words. The horse-faced envoy stepped forward from among the group of men. He smiled at me in a way I did not trust. "His Majesty says he has heard that the bear tolerates your presence in her cage," he said to me in Norse. "He desires to understand why this is, and if the bear is dangerous."

These were not simple questions. Why did the bear tolerate me? I could not truly say. "Your Majesty," I said. "I can only surmise—"

But the envoy broke in. "Is the bear dangerous?" he demanded.

Dangerous? Certainly, she was dangerous, but if the king judged her *very* dangerous, he might not allow her to venture outside her cage. "To some people, yes," I said, "but only if—"

Only if she feels threatened, I was going to say, which was not quite entirely true, but the envoy turned from me before I could fully explain; he began to speak to the king in French. The king frowned and furrowed his brow. The envoy went on, and it seemed to me that it couldn't possibly take so long to translate what little I had managed to say. I ventured a glance at the keeper. He looked worried.

The king said something to the envoy, who turned back to me. "What excuse do you have for the fact that the bear has fallen deathly ill while in your care?" he demanded.

Excuse? While in my care? Alarmed, I shot another glance at the keeper, whose demeanor had gone from worry to outright fear.

"She . . . I . . ." I swallowed hard. "I think she is sad. I think she misses her home. I think—"

Again, the envoy cut me off. He turned back to the king and spoke for so long that this time I was certain that he could not be translating what I had said, that he must be pouring his own notions into the king's ear, maybe lying outright. The king had begun to glower at me in a way that turned my bones to liquid. The keeper spoke up, now, but the king and the envoy both glared at him, and he ceased. The king spoke, briefly and harshly, and then the envoy wheeled upon me.

"Why did you steal His Majesty's bear?"

Steal? Steal the bear?

A dark surge of hopelessness engulfed me. There was nothing to be done. No matter what I said, he would twist my words, condemn me. No one else in the room could understand me; I might as well be mute. The bear . . . There was no help for her now. I had failed her.

I would be disgraced—or worse. Maybe put to death as a thief by the old enemy of my father. . . .

My father.

But wait.

Was it possible?

Might the king . . . speak Welsh?

The envoy repeated the question. "Why did you steal the bear?"

I turned to the king and began to answer him directly in my native tongue.

I had hoped to see comprehension in his face, but instead, his scowl deepened. The envoy honked out a loud protest, riding over my words. The keeper looked deeply sorrowful now; the words all left my mouth.

It was done.

The king turned to one side and spoke to his knot of retainers. One man peeled off from the group, said something to the king, and moved toward me. I didn't know if he was going to escort me from the room, or clap me in irons, or slit my throat on the spot. But he halted before me and said in perfect Welsh: "You speak as a born Welshman. Tell me who you are."

CHAPTER 52

To Be a Bear Again

I TOLD HIM my father's name, and my mother's. I told him the names of my father's father, and of his father, also. The Welshman said his name was Bevyn, and that he had known my father, though not well. He said he had bought a good horse from him. He told me he had heard that my mother had returned to Norway and had taken me with her. He told me he had heard that she had married again. I affirmed that all of this was true, and told him my stepfather's name.

"You and I will speak more of this anon," Bevyn told me. "But first, *did* you steal the bear?"

"The ship ran aground in a storm," I said. "I didn't

want the bear to drown in her cage, so I released her. I thought we could capture her later, if we survived, but if the ship went down, she would die."

"*Did* the ship go down?"

"Well, no, but I thought it was going to."

"Who can confirm your story?"

"Anyone who was aboard can tell of the storm and how we ran aground! The captain or the ship's doctor . . . Maybe they knew it wasn't as dire as I had feared, but . . ."

I could see doubt in Bevyn's eyes, though it seemed to me that he wanted to believe me. "Listen," I said, "there was another time, after the pirates, when the bear escaped and I led her back into her cage by myself. The entire crew saw."

"Pirates?"

"Yes, the bear saved us from them."

"You say that others witnessed this?"

"Yes!"

"This doctor and the captain . . . Are they in London still?"

"The doctor is. The captain, no."

Bevyn motioned me to wait, and then he turned to the king and spoke to him in French.

All eyes turned to me as he did so. The king's

countenance seemed to soften a bit and grow curious. The envoy, though—his face reddened, and he began to bleat, but the king silenced him with a gesture and a word.

The king spoke to Bevyn, who turned to me and said, "His Majesty requests to know how you came to be the keeper of the bear. He requests to hear of the pirates, and the shipwreck, and of the bear's escapes."

I told my tale up to the point when the captain took me on, leaving out that I had stolen the rabbit haunch. Nor did I tell about the running energy, or the humming, for I did not want the king to think me crackbrained. The king then prodded me to know what had befallen thereafter, and soon enough, I found myself skimming across the surface of the entire adventure. I made sure to tell how the bear had taken me to shore, and caught fish for me to eat, and protected me from the boars. I did not tell what was in my heart—that, in the end, I had wanted to free her—but I did say that I owed her a debt of honor and whatever aid I might provide.

When I had done, the king rested his chin on a fist, regarding me. He said something else, which Bevyn relayed: "And why does the bear refuse to eat now?"

"I don't know for certain," I said. "The doctor judges

it may be that her humors are out of balance, or she has a pollution of the blood. The keeper deems she might miss her home in the north."

The king said something, and Bevyn translated:

"What do *you* think?"

I hesitated, fearing that the king would take offense, for the bear was a gift to him, and he had a right to hold her. But the bear was dying, and it must be said. "I think it is the cage."

When Bevyn translated, the king nodded, seeming to ponder this without offense. And then he spoke again, and Bevyn translated back to me:

"His Majesty desires to know if you think that a daily swim in the river will make a difference to the bear."

Ah. So they had told him my idea. And he was, in fact, considering it! "I believe so," I said.

The king wanted to know if I was certain.

"No, Your Majesty," I owned.

The king wanted to know if I could lead the bear to the water without danger to myself and others and if I could persuade the bear to return to her cage.

I told him that I was hopeful that I could safely lead her to the water. And that I thought I could return her to her cage, but I wasn't wholly sure, as I had used food to entice her before, and now she did not want to eat. "But still," I said, "she often followed me with no food at all, when we were—" I almost said *free*, but stopped myself. "When we were lost in the Low Countries. And she is weaker now, Your Majesty. I think that two strong men with ropes could pull her back if she should balk or attempt to escape."

Now the envoy cut in again. The keeper tried to put in a word, but the envoy galloped on, whinnying like a spooked horse, and only ceased when the king interrupted.

After the king had finished saying his piece, Bevyn turned to me. "His Majesty says that the envoy reminds us that the bear is a gift from the Norwegian king, and that if she escapes or has to be destroyed, it will be disrespectful to King Haakon and unfavorable to relations between the two lands. And the envoy claims that *you* are not to be trusted because you set the bear at liberty, and by his reckoning, you will certainly try to do so again. And the Keeper of the Menagerie says that if something does not change, the bear will inevitably die. Given all of these circumstances, His Majesty seeks to know what you advise."

There was something odd about the way the king was looking at me. And it was likewise strange that he was asking for my counsel—for the second time. With that half-lidded eye, his face was hard to decipher. Was there something sly in it? Was this a trick of some kind?

But then I recalled a bit of gossip I had heard about this king. That he had been crowned when he was nine years old, upon the death of his father. That for many a year, others had made his choices for him, and that his nobles constrained him still. And I remembered how he had seemed before, when he had first laid eyes upon the bear. The sense of recognition, and of sorrow. I recalled how he had turned sharply away, as if it was painful to gaze on her for too long.

"As to escape," I replied, "I swear to you on my father's honor that I will not attempt it. And as to the rest . . . Since her capture the bear has been hemmed in on all sides by men who desire to use her for their own purposes. Noble purposes, to be sure, for she is a royal bear, and much honored in her native and adopted lands. And yet she is not free to be a bear and do the things that bears wish to do. And if she could, for a part of every day, have some time in which she could be a bear again . . . I believe she *might* decide to eat, and to live."

When this was relayed, the king leaned back in his

throne. He closed his eyes for a moment, then gazed up into the colored light that streamed in through the high stained-glass windows. The envoy flashed me a wrathful look, and the keeper quirked the corners of his mouth in a half smile. Some of the retainers shuffled, but no one spoke.

Then the king turned to the assembled company and made a final-sounding pronouncement, and I knew from his countenance that the answer was yes, even before Bevyn opened his mouth to speak.

CHAPTER 53

The River

WE WERE WAITING when they came.

I had slipped between the cage bars and buckled the new harness onto the bear. Now, leaning close, I breathed in the familiar musk of her and felt her warm, slow breath against me. She tensed, raising her head. In a moment, I heard voices. Outside the cage, the doctor and the keeper straightened and turned to face the western gate, where torchlight pricked the darkness.

Boots rang on the paving stones and then crunched in the frostbitten grass of the grove. I heard a jingling of chain mail, a clank of weapons. Moonlight bled through the web of black branches above and flowed like dappled waters across the advancing figures.

There were three of them, I saw—not two, as had been planned. I wondered if the envoy had changed his mind. He had said that he wanted no part of this, that he washed his hands of us entirely, that he would take no blame for the ill that would surely come of my misbegotten scheme.

I heard a rattling of quills from the direction of the prickly-beast's cage, and a soft grunt from the hump-backed horse. One of the big cats coughed. The bear made a sound so low I couldn't hear it, but rather felt it rumbling in her chest. I dug my fingers deep into the fur above one ear, and began to hum.

Now two of the men, wearing castle guards' livery, advanced and spoke to the keeper. The third man, cloaked and hooded, stood well back.

The guards threw coils of thick rope to the ground. The keeper unlocked the padlock and opened the cage door a crack. The guards moved to block the door, lest the bear should try to escape, while the keeper threaded the ends of the rope through the crack. I tied each end to the rings attached to the bear's harness, and tested the knots to make sure that they would hold.

The guards stepped away from the cage and stood

braced to either side. The keeper tugged on the door, and with a rusty moan, it swung wide.

The bear raised her nose to sniff the air. She made a little grunting sound and nuzzled my hair. I could feel a tautness in her, held like a question. But the thrumming, running energy . . . It was gone.

I recalled the last time the bear had stood at the threshold of an open cage door, when the pirates had attacked. But this was a different season. This was a different bear.

I stepped through the doorway and stood just outside the cage. "Come," I said to her. "Follow me."

A small breeze creaked in the brittle tree branches. The bear snorted. Slowly, she clambered to her feet. "Come," I said. She padded across the threshold to me. I hummed in her ear, then turned and began to walk across the dark, deserted grounds toward the ramp to the water gate.

Would she follow?

She hoisted her nose up into the air again and snuffled for so long, I feared she might stay there all night.

Come along, Bear!

Warily, she took a step in my direction, and then another.

The guards paid out their ropes and stood as far from the bear as they might. If she had truly wanted to escape, she *might* have done so—poor, starveling creature though she was. Even five or six muscle-bound men-at-arms of the garrison would have been no match for her in earlier days. But now, to my relief, she began to shuffle along behind me. The keeper, the doctor, and the hooded man followed.

When we came to the water gate, the guards tied the ropes to iron rings set in the stone walls to either side. One guard ratcheted up the great iron portcullis, with a harsh, rasping clatter. When he had done, both guards untied the knots from the wall rings and wrapped the ends of the ropes about their gloved hands.

And there we stood, with the whole of the Thames River before us and not a single bar to block the way.

The bear sniffed at the air again, shifting her weight from one side to another. She chuffed, sending up a plume of frozen breath. A sudden wind gust chilled my neck and made me shiver. The stars shone clear above us, and the moon made a bright, cold path across the Thames, and the city stood dim and far across the water. And I couldn't help but recall the season when we were alone and free, the bear and

I, out in the wild world together, with no master to command or restrain us.

A voice spoke behind us. When I turned to look, moonlight shone in upon the cloaked man's face, and I caught sight of a familiar, hooded eye.

Not the envoy—the king.

Then the keeper crunched across the sand to me. He glanced at the king and motioned me to make haste.

And I had been hoping she would go in of her own free will and that I wouldn't have to go with her, because by now the river had grown frigid. But I took off my fine new boots and stepped into the River Thames, braving the sudden shock of icy water. And my heart was knocking hard against my chest, because if the bear didn't follow soon, they would lead her back to her cage again, and she would never come out alive.

I waded out until the river reached my chest, burning cold like fire, until the waves licked and whispered at my ears. The bear lifted her nose in my direction and tasted the air. She took one pigeon-toed step and sniffed again.

I couldn't even hum; I held my breath.

Of a sudden, she seemed to gather herself up and,

with a great splash, plunged into the river. And now I felt the distant hum of the old running energy on her. She flowed through the water toward me, and I took her harness in both hands, and she was swimming, taking me with her.

And then, just for this moment, we were free.

A Note from the Author

THIS NOVEL IS based upon the true story of a "pale bear" given to King Henry III of England by King Haakon IV of Norway in 1251 or 1252.[1] The bear was kept in the menagerie of the Tower of London and was allowed to swim in the Thames River. She lived for many years.

I first read about the bear in Daniel Hahn's fascinating book, *The Tower Menagerie*, and I've been captivated by her ever since. We do know a few scant facts about this bear, but over the centuries, most of her story has been lost. How was she transported from Norway to London? Who took care of her? Who had the idea—and the courage— to let her out of her cage so that she could swim in the Thames River? Who gave permission for this dangerous plan, and why?

As far as possible I have remained true to what is known about the bear, but I have made up the rest of the story. In this note I will trace the line between what is known about

1. Some sources say 1251, for instance: Geoffrey Parnell, *The Royal Menagerie at the Tower of London* (London: Royal Armouries Museum, 1999), 5. Others say 1252, for instance: Daniel Hahn, *The Tower Menagerie* (New York: Penguin, 2003), 21.

the pale bear's journey . . . and what I have imagined.

While I refer to the bear as "she," the truth is that we don't know if the actual historical bear was male or female. In fact, we can't be absolutely certain that she was a polar bear, rather than a white strain of black bear, because in the Middle Ages, people didn't classify species as precisely as we do today, and the records are incomplete. According to Hahn, the only known reference to the bear's color may be found in a letter from Henry III, originally written in French and addressed to "the keeper of our pale [or *white*, depending upon the translation] bear, lately sent us from Norway, and which is in our Tower of London."[2] However, because the bear hailed from Norway, where polar bears are indigenous, I think it quite likely that she was a polar bear.

We know nothing about the bear's journey from Norway to London. I have surmised that she would have traveled on a type of ship known as a *keel*, typical of Scandinavian merchant vessels at the time of this story. Keels had a single deck on which the crew worked, cooked, ate, and slept. The bear cage would have been secured to the deck, as the ship's hold was very shallow and probably not entirely watertight; cargo stored below would have to be sealed in casks. When needful, sailors bailed by hand and by bucket.

Many keels had a sterncastle and/or a forecastle,

2. Hahn, 20.

which might have stood on wooden legs attached only to the deck or, increasingly with the passage of time, might have been built into and integrated with the sides of the ship. I have chosen the latter option for the *Queen Margrete*, dividing the space beneath the sterncastle into two rooms—the captain's quarters and a storeroom. The *Queen Margrete*'s tiller, which connects to a centered, rear rudder, runs through a gap between the rooms. We don't know for certain where sailors would have kept their seabags and sea chests; I have imagined that these would be stowed in the storeroom under the sterncastle.

In the thirteenth century, sea navigation was a dodgy enterprise, requiring much experience and skill on the part of sea captains. Compasses were not in general use, nor were the detailed sea charts of later times. Captains sailed within sight of land whenever possible, using their knowledge of landmarks, currents, the composition of the sea bottom, and the set of the sea swells to ascertain a ship's position.[3]

The bear arrived in London accompanied by her own keeper from Norway. We know nothing about this keeper; I have imagined that he might have been a twelve-year-old boy, as boys were expected to go to work earlier then than now. We do know that the keeper of the entire

---

3. For illustrations and more information about navigation and ships of this era, I recommend Robert Gardiner, ed., Reprint. *Cogs, Caravels, and Galleons: The Sailing Ship 1000-1650* (Annapolis: Naval Institute Press, 1994).

Tower menagerie was one William de Botton, who was probably a minor household official of the king and who would have been expected to do much of the dirty work of managing the menagerie.[4] It is unlikely that he had much special expertise with animals, save for what he learned on the job.

In any case, the sheriffs of the City of London provided a daily allowance toward the pale bear's keep, and soon, at the king's request, they invested in a muzzle and an iron chain ("to hold the bear without the water") and a long, strong cord ("to hold the same bear fishing or washing . . . in the river Thames").[5] Feeding the bear must have been expensive; possibly it was believed that if the bear could shift for herself, she would be cheaper to keep. The sheriffs also paid for a thick wrap for the bear's keeper, who, for reasons that are not entirely clear, was expected to accompany the bear on her fishing expeditions.[6]

In the Middle Ages, kings often kept collections of exotic animals, frequently gifts from other monarchs. Henry III's great-grandfather, Henry I, kept an assortment of such animals at his manor in Woodstock, near Oxford. According to chronicler William of Malmesbury, they included lions, leopards, lynxes, camels, and a porcupine.[7]

4. This and the following sentence are per Hahn, 29.
5. Hahn, 21. Also in Phillip Drennon Thomas, "The Tower of London's Royal Menagerie," *History Today* 46:8 (1996): 30.
6. Hahn, 21-2.
7. Hahn, 13.

At some point, probably during the reign of King John (1199–1216), a private collection of animals was begun at the Tower of London,[8] and the whole Woodstock menagerie was transported to the Tower sometime in 1252.[9] We don't know precisely what kinds of animals resided in the menagerie when the pale bear lived there. For the purposes of this story, I have put in all of King Henry I's animals (though surely the originals had died by 1252). Additionally, taking full advantage of artistic license, I have embroidered in a peacock.

It is uncertain exactly where the menagerie was kept within the complex of the Tower of London at the precise time of this story. To complicate matters, the Tower was under major construction then, parts of the western wall having collapsed in 1240, and again in 1241. In 1253, the western wall was still breached, and as late as 1253, the repairs and reconstruction continued.[10] I have imagined that the animals were kept in cages in the outer bailey, in what was then a stand of trees—but I'm just guessing. Apparently, by the beginning of the fourteenth century, there may have been a *berehaus*, which would have located the bear's quarters in the inner ward, near Henry's private chambers.[11] But perhaps the *berehaus* was for the brown

8. Parnell, *Menagerie*, 2; and Hahn, 16.
9. Hahn, 18.
10. Edward Impey and Geoffrey Parnell, *The Tower of London* (London: Merrell, 2000), 29.
11. Hahn, 32.

bears that came to live in the Tower menagerie years after our bear was gone; I have chosen to keep the bear of our story in the grove with the rest of the animals.

On the other hand, it's somewhat easier to surmise where the bear might have spent her days when chained near the Thames River. If you visit the Tower of London today, you will see a sculpture of the bear on the spot where she was most likely tethered.

Some readers may doubt whether our bear might have been able to catch fish, because polar bears are so specialized for hunting seals on ice. While it is known that polar bears eat eggs and birds and seaweed during summer ice melts, it's unlikely that they could obtain sufficient nourishment that way year-round, and the prospect of our polar bear catching fish from a river, as grizzly bears do, might seem highly implausible. And yet I have seen contemporary photographs, videos, and anecdotal accounts of salmon-fishing polar bears, and some early explorers of Newfoundland witnessed and wrote about polar bears that caught fish, as well—John Cabot in 1497, and Captain George Cartwright around 1770.[12] It is heartbreaking that this alien skill is unlikely to save polar bears if too much polar ice melts. But the evidence is sufficient to make me believe that this one particular ice bear *might* have fished

12. Andrew E. Derocher, *Polar Bears: A Complete Guide to their Biology and Behavior* (Baltimore: Johns Hopkins University Press, 2012), 88.

for salmon in the Low Countries and on the banks of the River Thames.

I like to imagine her outside the confines of her cage, lolling on the riverbank beyond the Tower walls and bathing or fishing at her leisure. I like to imagine Arthur donning his "thick wrap" and swimming far out into the river with her—not in order to prevent her escape, but because he treasured the moments of freedom they had together. I like to imagine the citizens of thirteenth-century London navigating their ships and fishing boats and ferries around their resident pale bear, struck with awe at her magnificence, even as they knew she would not be with them forever.

Acknowledgments

I AM INDEBTED to the generosity of so many who helped me with this book!

Oregon Zoo curator Amy Cutting was one of the first people to hear the story I intended to tell. She answered my questions about polar bears by e-mail and in person, shared her extensive knowledge and experience, vetted the entire manuscript, and recommended reputable resources. Better yet, she invited me "backstage" at the zoo to meet, up close, the venerable and astonishing polar bears Conrad and Tasul. I watched as the fifteen-hundred-pound Conrad gently lipped a grape from Cutting's palm, and saw the bears respond as Cutting and keeper Amy Hash fed them fish and conversed with them—with words on one side of the colloquy and a combination of rumbles, grunts, and gestures on the other. Cutting and Hash answered more questions on the spot, and Hash treated me to an unforgettable lesson in polar bear vocalizations. At that time, Conrad and Tasul were some of the oldest polar bears in captivity and also, no doubt, some of the oldest polar bears on the planet. They are with us no longer, but they served as inspiration for my bear throughout the writing process.

My husband, historian Dr. R. J. Q. Adams, scoured the archives for articles about the Tower of London menagerie at the time of this story, yielding new insights and more clearly defining for me the line between what is known and what remains unknown. He has supported the creation of this book in ways great and small, including addressing a multitude of questions about historical research and documentation.

Maritime historian Dr. Lawrence V. Mott answered a long list of questions about ships of this time and place, transforming my understanding of the sea voyage in the book; he also recommended helpful resources. Historian Dr. James Bradford was invaluable as well in advancing my knowledge of medieval ships.

The press office and curators of the Tower of London answered myriad questions before my visit, and the Tower guides answered yet more when I was there, lending much to my understanding of the menagerie and the history of the Tower.

Dr. Eric and Doris Kimmel sent me wonderful photos, a book, and additional information on medieval Bergen, Norway. Jan Albrecht also sent me great photos and material on Bergen.

I'm so grateful to all the members of my Oregon critique group for their friendship, support, and insight on the book. Special thanks to Kathi Appelt, Marion Dane

ACKNOWLEDGMENTS

Bauer, Pamela Smith Hill, and Ellen Howard, who took time to read the manuscript, and whose wise and generous responses helped me to improve the story immeasurably. Over the past couple of years, Marion and Kathi have nurtured my life as a writer in ways I can never repay. Many thanks to Rose Eder, Dr. Kelly Fletcher, and Diane Linn, who also took time to read the manuscript, and whose kind and perceptive comments enlightened and sustained me.

Heartfelt thanks to my brilliant editor, Karen Wojtyla, for her faith in and enthusiasm for the project, which mean more to me than I can express, and for her supersmart notes and comments. Many thanks as well to editorial assistant Nicole Fiorica for her good cheer and patience while answering my many questions and for shepherding the project through. And I'm very grateful to copyeditor Jeannie Ng for her careful reading and great skill.

Finally, to my extraordinary agent, Rubin Pfeffer, for his belief in the book and for his wisdom, trust, counsel, and care—my profound appreciation.

Thank you, one and all!